A Search for the Unknown

The Wyvern's Guild, Volume 1

Jazlynn Dickens

Published by Jazlynn Dickens, 2024.

This is a work of fiction. Similarities to real people, places, or events are entirely coincidental.

A SEARCH FOR THE UNKNOWN

First edition. June 1, 2024.

Copyright © 2024 Jazlynn Dickens.

ISBN: 979-8227551221

Written by Jazlynn Dickens.

Table of Contents

A Search for the Unknown

Chapter 1

Gilbert Pridestone, a low life as some would say, strolled through the rundown streets of Hadune, the city of scoundrels. The city had many names yet that was the one that most people agreed upon.

The city once flourished with bright flowers, glowing and clean streets with its main occupants being highborn and noble people that now lived in the upper city. Now it was not so bright.

During the Crown war when refugees needed a place to go, Hadune, being known for despising the lowborn, had no choice but to let them take residence in the once great city.

That was far before Gilbert's time, now the rest of the streets were filled with the unfortunate, poor, and lowborn people, yearning for the life of the royals and nobles.

Gilbert rather liked it, though. It wasn't the place to expect a warm welcome, or even a smile from a passerby. Everyone scowled at each other, the streets were crawling with pickpockets, slavers and their slaves, there could have even been a few murderers walking the streets, but to Gilbert, it was home.

Gilbert had short curly, dark brown hair matched with round brown eyes, almost like coffee without milk, and was wearing his usual crimson red tailcoat, dark trousers and blue vest over his tunic. He usually wore rather simple things, except for the expensive necklace he wore under his velvet scarf, it had a silver dragon with an emerald for an eye pendant on it. He had his usual leather belt on, that had crossbow bolts strapped to it, that went to two mini, four-shot crossbows. There was a small lever by the trigger that rotated and loaded another bolt. Gilbert was the fastest sharpshooter there was, in his opinion.

He glanced at the Mug and Crow; it was one of the most popular inns. He wasn't sure why, it looked just like every other place in Hadune, run down and falling apart.

He slipped down an alleyway, took a left and there it was, The Red Wyvern, the biggest tavern in all of Hadune. Gilbert worked there, or rather lived there. His boss was Eric Dustmark, A highborn that was cut off from his family and forced onto the streets. Now he owns the best tavern in the city.

Gilbert walked onto the porch where two older men were guarding the door.

"Gents." He said with a warm smile.

"You're late, Pridestone. Boss isn't happy." One of them growled. Gilbert waved him off and walked through the door saying:

"He can't stay mad at me, you know that."

The tavern was all wood, creating a welcoming ambience, and filled to the brim with people. A band was playing upbeat music with barmaids going from table to table. The stage was to the right of the door, the bar was to the left. The rest of the room was covered in tables. Wooden columns attached to the rafters did come down in between a few tables, but that's where the lights were, so people didn't seem to notice some of them landed in the walkway. Gilbert walked through it to the back of the room across from the door, where Eric was waiting for him.

He wore a black fancy trench coat, black trousers, and a black vest with golden buttons over a dark gray shirt.

He had an expensive taste, and it showed. He had short, dirty blonde hair. Tall, dark, and intimidating, He had his signature cane, not that he needed one. It was something from his grandfather, the handle was black with a silver dragon on the top.

It was made like Gilbert's pendant with a diamond for the eye. Gilbert took a seat next to him and fixed his eyes on the band.

"Gilbert, we were supposed to meet half an hour ago." Smooth and commanding, Eric's voice may have been the most intimidating thing about him. Not to Gilbert, not anymore at least.

When Gilbert was younger, he'd ended up begging on the streets after his parents died and he'd aged out of his orphanage, Eric found him and offered him a job in The Red Wyvern. He promised riches galore if he hung around. They'd been like brothers ever since.

"I was on a... erm... personal business venture. You don't pay me for nothing y'know." Gilbert replied as a barmaid placed two tankards of ale on the table.

"I've told you a thousand times, buying people drinks won't make you friends." Eric said, turning his attention away from the band and looking at Gilbert with penetrating brown eyes. "Nothing in this rotten city will."

"I only bought a few rounds. you know I'm not *that* careless, and it was only for some fun."

"It's risky, Gil, I've told you that." Eric sighed and shook his head. "But I didn't ask you here to talk about your drinking issues, it's about a job." Gilbert rose in his seat and raised his eyebrows.

They didn't just gain income from the tavern, they took odd jobs, the last one they had was months ago and it was about retrieving some family heirloom from some thieves. It didn't seem like their employer was telling the truth, but their job was to do what they were paid to do, not ask questions.

"A man named Arloon Musiak, needs us to find an.... Artifact of sorts." Eric shifted uncomfortably and looked back at the stage.

"Ric, what's wrong?" Gilbert laid a hand on his shoulder.

"It's a lost cause, but it's necessary. He wants us to find-" Eric was cut off by a barmaid who hustled over to him. "Sorry sir, but there's a woman looking for you. Unfortunately, it isn't a lovely one either. Helga Honostone." She said, handing Eric a piece of paper.

"Great, what does that hag want now?" Gilbert said, trying to read over Eric's shoulder. Eric folded it closed again, stood up and started for the door. "I'll take care of it, Gilbert. We'll talk later."

Chapter 2

Gilbert

Gilbert slipped through crowds of people, made it to the bar

and sat down. He drummed his finger on the pommel of his crossbow.

Why was Eric worried? What was the job? Why was it necessary? What

does the old hag Helga want now?

Gilbert's multiple questions were interrupted by something small pelting the back of his head. He turned his head, no one was there, no one was even facing him.

"You know thinking isn't a good look for you. So why do it?" A voice said from above.

Gilbert looked up to find himself looking at Ryker Thorne, a half-elf, half-human, sitting in the rafters.

Ryker wore his usual navy-blue assassin gear, with a dark blue cloak draped over one of his shoulders and wrapped around his neck. He also had a necklace with a charm like Gilbert's, but it had sapphire for an eye. Ryker wore fingerless gloves and had a bunch of knives, most of them were concealed but he had two knives strapped to each of his thighs and four knives on his belt.

He had silvery platinum hair tied back in a long braid that went down to his ankles, he had shorter strands that went just past his chin in the front that hung loose. Gilbert sometimes couldn't comprehend the fact that his hair was so long, and how well it matched his dark blue eyes.

He was small built and seemed to appear randomly whenever and wherever he wanted. Yet the strangest thing about him was his markings. The tips of his ears were bright blue and there were four dots underneath his eyes, some elven thing apparently. Another elven thing was his earrings that decorated the points of his ears. He was also in Eric's inner circle. They called themselves the Fangs

Ryker had a handful of pumpkin seeds he was munching on, he offered one to Gilbert.

"Want some? They are delicious."

"Ryker, you know Helga is here, right?" Gilbert pointed out as he watched Ryker toss a pumpkin seed into his mouth and crunched.

"Is that what's bothering you?" He asked nonchalantly. Gilbert's eyes widened and his temper rose. *Because that sounds like something someone who was treated so horribly would say.* Gilbert thought.

"Me?! *You're* the one who should be panicking. For all we know she could be here to take you back!" Gilbert exclaimed.

Ryker always knew what to say or do to get Gilbert riled up. Though it was fair to say Gilbert had a short fuse and Ryker didn't help, he needed to get a better grip on it. Ryker just blinked at him seemingly not in the present anymore, rather in the past.

Helga Honostone was a rich, cruel, brat to put it nicely. She worked in a slave business, she bought kids, treated them horribly and trained them as assassins to be sold to the public. She brought them up in a place called The Silver Chalice, it was probably one of the most prominent businesses, as seemingly no one had a sense of decency.

Seeing as Ryker was a half elf, and elves were few and far between. Bounty hunters often tracked full-bloods and collected bounties. Because of that, a lot of sick people would pay thousands to have a part elf to parade around.

Ryker still wasn't fully paid for either, so it was no wonder she hounded Eric so much about fulfilling the payment. Which was probably why she was here now, technically Ryker was still her property and she never let him forget it.

According to what Ryker told them, His parents sold him to Helga when he was eight, leaving him with just a pocket watch that he often toyed with.

"I think you should learn to relax a bit and to take a joke, sure it was horrible, but it taught me what I know." Ryker shrugged.

"You really are wiser than your years." Gilbert remarked, rolling his eyes.

Ryker was the youngest of the group at eighteen. Gilbert was a close second at twenty and Eric, who acted like their older brother, was twenty-three.

Ryker hopped off the rafter beam and landed softly in front of Gilbert.

"I know right? I'm actually a genius." Gilbert grinned at him. They both knew Helga hardly taught anything school related. Ryker barely knew basic arithmatic. "Now, Eric said he had a job, but refused to discuss it with me without you. Has he told you anything?"

Gilbert nodded again and motioned for Ryker to follow him. The two passed through plenty of different people on their way, not one of them gave a friendly glance toward Ryker, only scowls and other dirty looks, which Gilbert gladly returned. Gilbert and Ryker sat down at Eric's personal table.

"I understand why you don't like people."

"I like people just fine. People just don't me." An older barmaid walked by the table and Gilbert stopped her.

"A bottle of brandy and a coffee, if you don't mind Anne." Anne glanced at Ryker then back and Gilbert.

"Eric's got the two of you running in circles, huh? Comin' right up." The people who worked at the wyvern were practically the only humans that didn't despise Ryker.

"I'm eighteen, Gil." Ryker asked, resting his chin on his arms.

"And?"

"And I can get my own coffee. Now tell me about this job."

Chapter 3

"A little more time is all I'm asking for, Helga." Eric pleaded,
they stood in an alleyway between the Red Wyvern and some silk shop
that he never bothered to pay attention to.

"You said that last month. Yet he still hasn't been paid off. I'm
starting to think you plan to smuggle him out of the city." Helga fanned
herself with her golden fan.

She wore an expensive creamy yellow gown that had a plunging
neckline with her auburn hair tied up in a bun with beads to
accessorize. She most definitely got it from selling people like Ryker, it
twisted Eric's stomach.

"That isn't what I'm planning. I just don't have the money yet, but
I will soon. Two more months Helga, please." Eric hated begging for
anything, but in this case, he made an exception.

Helga was evil, she had no mercy or sympathy for the kids that
she owned, no matter the age. Eric wasn't going to let Ryker slip back
into her hands. She was a puppet master pulling the strings of all the
assassins or spies she trained before they were sold.

Helga used them to thin the competition, many of her assassins
killed other slave traders for her without getting caught, that's how they
were trained. Although Ryker could kill now, he'd said he hadn't killed
anyone while working for the chalice.

Ryker used to be her prized pet, her best spy, her favorite tool,
he wasn't a person to her. She could order him to spy, frame, kidnap,
torture, Ryker was good at everything, so naturally he'd also become a
handy asset to Eric.

"Why should I trust you? How can you prove that you'll have the money then?" Helga's hazel eyes narrowed. "He's my prized pet Mister Dustmark. If you can't afford him perhaps you should turn him back over to me, we can sort out a different arrangement, I have many cheaper spies."

"No!" Eric snapped. "I just need two more months; I have a job in the works that will clear the debt."

"Hm. *One* more month, that's all Mister Dustmark." Helga walked back to where two small built men were waiting; they were assassins, like Ryker.

What am I going to do? He made his way out of the alleyway and back into the Red Wyvern. He spied Ryker and Gilbert talking at his personal table. Avoiding either of them seeing him, he slipped behind the counter and into the busy kitchen.

Eric glided easily around the chefs and waiters until he made it to the back wall. He held up his cane to it and muttered an incantation. The glowing green outline of a door appeared. He tapped the outline with his staff and the wall opened revealing spiral stairs that led upwards.

It was Eric's personal chambers, a magical room hidden in the walls of the Wyvern. There were other entry points such as windows, but no one except him and his inner circle knew about it. Plus, the charms on their necklaces were the only way they could find the door and get in. It was where he kept the vault, his office, and his bedroom.

He climbed the stairs as the wall closed behind him. When he made it to the top, he muttered another incantation and fire came from the cane, lighting all the candles in the room, creating an inviting ambience to the room.

His desk was in the middle of the room, off to a smaller room on the side was where his bed was. He leaned his cane on the wall beside the door and strolled over to a portrait of his grandfather that hung above his desk. Eric lifted it off the wall to reveal the vault.

He entered the combination and swung the vault door open. The inside was less than disappointing, most of the money went to supplies, staff and taxes, the leftover wasn't even close to paying off Ryker. He sighed, shut the vault and hung the picture of his grandfather back up.

Taking a seat at his desk he found himself looking at his grandfather's cane, thinking about his family. *Maybe, if I could contact them, they could pay for Ryker. Perhaps they feel guilty for cutting me off.* Eric scoffed. *As if I need their help. If they actually loved me they wouldn't have kicked me out.* He argued with himself until he heard the distinct noise the magical door made when it opened. Gilbert appeared in the doorway.

"Where's Ryker?" Eric asked. Gilbert shrugged and glanced behind him. "I don't know. He must've slipped out. You know I can't keep track of him. What did she want now?" Gilbert Leaned up against the door frame and crossed his arms.

"I only have one month to pay for him otherwise he goes back." Eric admitted. Gilbert just shook his head.

"How disappointing." Another voice said. Both Gilbert and Eric jumped and turned toward it. It was Ryker standing in front of the now open window.

"How do you do that?!" Demanded Gilbert. Ryker just shrugged and turned his attention back to Eric.

"So, is this job going to save me from going back or should I make a break for it?" Eric sighed

"Arloon wants us to find a dragon egg."

Chapter 4

Ryker froze, his brain went blank. Dragons went extinct hundreds of years ago during the crusade of divine wrath, finding an egg was a fool's errand. Dragons hadn't even been mentioned in any recent scroll or tome.

He fiddled with his pocket watch in his jeans pocket; it was the only thing his parents left him with after they sold him.

"I'm sorry, a what?" Gilbert asked. "Aren't dragons dead?"

"They are." Eric nodded. "Which makes this even more of a problem, but it's huge money. Six million gold pieces. It would be enough to pay Helga and still have plenty left over for renovations on the Wyvern."

Ryker just blinked at him. *I am going back to the chalice. I have no doubt.*

Memories flashed into his head, being chained to his bed so he couldn't escape, early morning, strenuous training for years on end and dozens of rules. If any were broken it was met with cruel retribution. One of which was Helga's cane made of heavy solid gold, the cane of punishment she called it, she used it to beat kids when they messed up. Ryker had been on the receiving end more times than he could count. He remembered one specific occasion a few months after he was sold.

He'd made an escape attempt; he managed to get a few blocks away from the gate of the city when one of Helga's goons had caught him and dragged him back. When Helga heard about it, she wasn't happy.

She'd beaten Ryker until he physically couldn't get off the floor and couldn't train for weeks. Sometimes at night he swore he still felt the pound of the cane in his ribs.

He closed his eyes and shook his head. *That isn't going to happen again, Eric wouldn't let it. Gilbert wouldn't let it.*

He moved from toying with his watch and rubbed the plaits of his braid between his fingers, almost counting them.

"Have we at least got a lead on where to look?" Ryker asked. *If Eric has a plan for this, I'll be fine.*

"He's told me about a book, the Tome of Kamika, that explains about a clutch of eggs that went missing before the crusade. If we can get that book, we may have an idea where to go." Eric thumbed through the pages of a different book on his desk. *We're chasing fairytales. I'd bet there is a saying about that.* He grabbed the end of his braid and started spinning it in circles. He didn't fully mean too; it was more of a comforting reflex.

Gilbert drew one of his crossbows. "Sounds easy enough, we get that book, find a clutch of dragon eggs, take one, return it to the creepy guy and boom just like that Ryker's free and I can finally get a proper bed rather than sleeping in a cot."

"Old man Gil is hurting his back without the luxury of a proper bed." Ryker sniggered as he draped his braid back over his shoulder. Poking fun at Gilbert was always calming.

"What can I say?" Gilbert grinned "I'm not as durable as you half elves."

"It's not that easy, Gil. The book is in one of the colleges in the upper city. The Oracle College, where the princess attends, so naturally it's got top notch security during the day." Eric explained, interlocking his fingers and resting his elbows on the desk

"That's why you have me." Ryker said proudly, he pulled a knife from his coat and thumbed the edge. "How many are we talking at night?"

"Too many, it will have to be an in and out venture quiet, quick, and precise." Eric tapped his foot against the floor. "Lucky for us, I've been thinking of a plan. And I've got it mostly worked out."

Chapter 5

Ryker

Ryker stood atop a cathedral in the upper city, one hand was wrapped around one of the thin poles that lined the top of each tower the other hand was gripping the duffle bag that Gilbert gave him.

His keen eyes could see all the way down to the main gate, where Gilbert and Eric were trying to get in disguised as noblemen.

Hadune was broken into two sections, after the crown wars the king put up a wall smack in the middle of the city to separate the nobles from the peasants. His heirs have kept the tradition going by not letting anyone from the lower city in.

Hours ago, Ryker had slipped over the wall, scouted out where the Oracle college was and scaled the cathedral to make sure Eric and Gil got in without issue.

The plan was for Ryker to get in and get out while Eric and Gilbert distracted the guards by posing as lost noblemen. It wasn't very well thought out compared to some of Eric's other heists, but time was short. After a few minutes the gate opened, and Eric and Gil strolled on through.

Perfect. Ryker slid down the rounded cathedral roof and hopped from building to building until he dropped into an unoccupied alleyway not far from the college.

"That's preposterous!" A voice called from the street.

Ryker slunk back into the shadows. It was a drunk and one of his friends coming out of what Ryker guessed was a tavern. *Fanciest tavern I've ever seen.*

"I'm telling you; they raised the price for elven ears. I wager those filthy bounty hunters will even start going after half elves." The other man said.

Rykers hand found one of his many knives he kept hidden in his assassin's garb. *I'd like to see them try. And what kind of drunk talks so fancy?* The two men walked out of sight.

Ryker stayed hidden; out of everything Ryker was good at he excelled at stealth. Ryker pulled up his hood, tucked his braid into it the best he could, but some of it still ran across his chest. He pulled his mask over his nose and checked the streets. There were only a few common people and two guards, but each of them had their backs turned.

With the grace of a cat Ryker dashed across the street only to hide in the shadows of the alley across from him.

"Did you hear something?" A guard asked.

"No. Why?" Another one said. He heard footsteps walking toward the alleyway. "I think you've had one too many, pal."

The footsteps stopped then became distant and then he heard chuckling. *Idiots, the whole lot of them.*

Even though they had the best education available in Hadune, the nobles weren't clever enough to know the streets. They thought like a highborn, not like a lowborn, leaving them defenseless against the real world outside their bubble.

Ryker climbed on some crates and eyed the ledge; it was far too high for him to jump. He reached into his pocket and pulled out his grappling hook. It was enchanted and made specially for assassins trapped in the chalice.

It looked like a small spearhead but when he twisted the bottom the end of a rope peeked out and sharp spikes jutted out of the flat sides. After pulling the rope to its full extent he flung it around the chimney on the roof. The rope tightened around the chimney by itself.

Ryker smirked thinking, *one thing about the chalice, they knew how to enchant gadgets.* Silent, useful, and effortless; that's how everything in the chalice was made.

After he made it on the roof, he unhooked the grappling hook and retracted the spikes. Easily he leaped from rooftop to rooftop, nearly falling on the wider gaps. He spotted the college. It was an ivory building like a cathedral but smaller. There was a glass canopy between the four spires. *I suppose that's one way in and out.* It had a black metal fence separating its garden from the apartment that Ryker was on.

Big jump. Ryker thought. He took a few steps back then dashed toward it. He made the leap.

He missed the roof but managed to catch himself on the ledge.

Dangling dangerously twenty feet above a bush that looked like poison ivy. *No, no, no!* His feet were clawing at the wall desperate for some kind of footing when he heard

"Did you hear something?"

Chapter 6

Rykers heart was beating in his throat, his fingers ached, and a million scenarios rushed through his head. *I could just drop and make a break for it. I could try to fight them. If I pulled myself up now, they would see me.*

He'd managed to gather his feet under him on the wall, but the footsteps came closer and the light from their lanterns crept around the corner.

"Excuse me!" Another voice called. "Would either of you know where the ivory palace is?" The footsteps stopped. One moment, then two, then three. Ryker's fingers cramped more and more each second. The footsteps started up again, walking away. The light disappeared around the corner again.

Ryker pulled himself up and flexed his aching fingers. He climbed across the roof and when he made it to the canopy, he started picking the padlock that was latched to the window.

"Alright thank you, I'm sorry but my cousin and I were ordered there by the king, and we've never been before." Ryker heard the other voice say in the poshest voice he'd ever heard. If he had to guess, that would be Gilbert. It was difficult not to laugh at how absurd he sounded.

Click! The padlock opened. He removed it and pushed the window open. Ryker pulled out his grappling hook again, sent the rope down and hooked the top to the roof. Once he glided down the rope, he took in his surroundings.

It was a glorious main room with plenty of columns and sofas. There were plenty of corridors and different doors.

Ryker stayed in the shadows as he made his way through the halls. *Where am I supposed to go from here?*

Keeping close to the wall, Ryker spotted a huge door that had a sign that said *'library'* above it. *Hah, it's almost like fate. I suppose it would be stupid to not keep a book in a library just because it's technically a tome.* He thought. *Wait, aren't they the same thing, or am I just dumb? Blasted Chalice not giving me proper education.*

Ryker enjoyed blaming all of his faults on the chalice. Although he wouldn't consider himself dumb, he wasn't exactly the brightest and spelling especially wasn't his strong suit.

"Stick with what you know. Besides we've got Eric he's got the brains, and he needs all the brawn he can get." Gilbert had said.

Ryker entered the library, inside there were hundreds of bookshelves filled with books. They were organized by type of book; history, mathematics, animals, and so forth. He sauntered over to the history section and started scanning the books that were organized by letter. *Tome of Kamika, would that be under T or K?*

He found the K section and scanned through the books. One of the biggest books said 'Kamika' in big bold letters. It was the only thing close to what they needed. He grabbed it and stuffed it in his bag.

Afterwards he made his way back to the rope and pulled himself back up to the roof, panting. His shoulders burned and ached by the time he was finished.

He glanced back at the inn he originally jumped from, he didn't want to take that risk again, but the deal was to meet back at the tavern after dawn which was still a few hours away.

Ryker thought back to earlier, when Helga first appeared, she hadn't just wanted to talk to Eric. One of the other assassins that Ryker knew personally gave him a note from her. Which was why he wasn't concerned when Gilbert said something about Helga

It didn't give him much, it was just a drawing of the silver chalice emblem, which usually meant trouble. Helga probably wanted to kill off someone who made her angry, or it could have been a threat, the good old "I have assassins you don't." routine. *Can't she get one of her other pets to do it?* Ryker thought angrily as he stuffed the note back in his pocket.

With one hand he toyed with his braid, with the other he fiddled with his father's watch again, for some reason he found it comforting. He still remembered when his father gave it to him, however his face was blurred in all Rykers memories.

Begrudgingly, Ryker took the same route from which he came in, nearly falling on the same leap. After scaling the wall back to the rundown streets of Hadune, he strolled through, silent as a cat, ignoring all the hateful and rude glances he got from the people.

He focused more on the other businesses, inns, taverns, stores. The filthy streets brought him comfort. Though it was dark gloomy, and filled with scammers, liars, slavers, and probably a few murderers, it was home.

That was until he turned onto the street the chalice was on. *Here we go.*

Chapter 7

"Why do we have to wait so long?" Gilbert groaned. "Ryker

has it, I'm positive." Eric gave him an annoyed look.

They made their escape a few minutes ago, obviously they were interrogated at the gates. Eric explained that they got the dates wrong, and the king was expecting them the next week. It got them through the gates, but still something nagged in Eric's stomach, a sinking feeling about Ryker.

Was he worried? He'd gotten the same feeling about Gilbert a few times, but never about Ryker, he could fend for himself. Why did he care so much about his employees? Eric tried to stuff those feelings down.

"I know that look. It's the worried boss look. Ryker got it, I'm sure. Perhaps it's these stuffy clothes. They're suffocating." Gilbert had a point, the clothes were suffocating, of course, Eric had worn this type of clothing before he was kicked out.

Either way, it wasn't about if Ryker got the book or not, it was about his safety and a little bit about his loyalties.

Eric bought him, so by law Ryker belonged to Eric, but that wasn't how Eric saw it, then again, he wasn't quite sure what Ryker was to him. He wasn't that trusting of anyone who wasn't Gilbert.

He saw Ryker more as an asset than property. It didn't help that seeing as Eric was paying him off and he would technically belong to Eric, so he wouldn't get paid. What if Ryker thought that Eric saw him how Helga did? An object, nothing more. Eric may be cruel to him at times, but he still saw him as a person.

By the time they made it back to the Wyvern dawn was only an hour away. Although it was late the band still played and there were still plenty of people there, most drunkards spent all night in the tavern and returned home at dawn. The break between first light and midday was when they closed the shop, and all the night shift staff went home. They had enough staff to keep it open all the time, but business was always slow, and it was easier on the day shift to come in later rather than sooner.

Eric started for his chamber, but Gilbert caught him by the elbow.

"We've got time. Let's sit and enjoy the ambience, we can change once Ryker comes back. I don't want to fall asleep before I know he's okay and these clothes will definitely keep me awake." Eric nodded as Gilbert pulled him back to his table.

After a few minutes someone joined them, Eric turned, expecting to see Ryker, but it was someone else. Shoulder length dark brown hair with a matching beard wearing a casual suit with two bodyguards behind him.

Eric recognized him immediately, it was Arloon Musiak.

"Mister Dustmark, I'm here to talk business. Is this ...lowlife your associate or your attendant?" Arloon questioned smugly.

He and Arloon were practically the same person, or at least they used to be. Before Eric was cut off from his family he would've seen Gilbert the same way, a lowlife or a bum. Gilbert scoffed and looked between Eric and Arloon.

"This is Gilbert Pridestone, my companion and partner." Eric explained. "Gilbert, this is Arloon Musiak." Arloon looked surprised, but then it faded into more of a pitying look.

"My apologies, I'm rather old school. Not used to seeing a highborn and a lowborn mingling, but I understand not being able to afford proper associates, with your family and all." Gilbert glared at him.

"Eric, I'm not sure we should agree to this. I mean, with Ryker being…. Well Ryker." Eric scowled at him.

"Ryker? Who's Ryker? Why wasn't I informed of either of these people? I should be informed of everyone working this job." Arloon looked suspiciously between them. Obviously Arloon didn't know how things worked in the lower city.

When you hire someone, you don't get a say on who the person you hire works with. In the upper city you're able to meet everyone and decide who you want to work with, and hours of pleasantries are exchanged before business. In the lower city your options are limited to practically nothing.

"Things are different here in the lower city, Mister Musiak. It's just us three. At the minute Ryker is…. Ryker is well…. Missing in action." Gilbert explained. "But he has your book." Arloon raised his eyebrows at Eric.

"You allowed one of your associates to run off with the book?" Eric pinched the bridge of his nose and shook his head. *Gilbert, can't you shut up for two seconds?*

"Ryker tends to disappear, yes. But don't fear he's going to bring us the book at dawn." Arloon shook his head.

"Have we somewhere else to wait for him? In private, perhaps."

Gilbert and Eric locked eyes, it was clear they were thinking the same thing. Something was off about him; he wasn't quite sure about trusting him, not with his bodyguards at least.

"We do, but they will have to wait outside." Eric shifted his focus back to Arloon. He gave Eric a perplexed look then glanced between his bodyguards then back at Eric.

"Ryker gets uneasy around too many people. If he sees so many he may not show up." Gilbert explained, nodding at him. *Gilbert can lie? I'm shocked.* Eric hadn't realized how good Gilbert was at lying, Ryker was rather social, when people weren't glaring at him, but it was a good excuse for the time being.

"Hm, is your associate a mouse, Mister Dustmark?" Eric couldn't help but snicker. One could say Ryker was as quiet as a mouse, but that would be an understatement. Eric guessed mice watched his feet to learn his technique.

"Quite the opposite, Mister Musiak. Gilbert can show them out. You can come with me."

Chapter 8

Ryker

Ryker found himself frozen outside the door of the chalice.

He knew he needed to go in, but his hand was stuck hovering above

the door handle. He knew that there wasn't much Helga could do to

him, not with his contract to Eric, but there wasn't exactly a line she

wouldn't cross if it meant she'd feel better. *Just get through this and you*

can forget about it later.

He forced himself to detach from his emotions. After a minute or two he just felt numb, almost like he wasn't really there. As if he was watching someone else through their own eyes.

He opened the door and walked into the chalice, he still had roughly an hour before he had to go back to the wyvern.

The main room was inviting, but it also brought back many childhood memories. Being brought there for beatings when Helga was angry, sometimes her goons would get tired of watching them and would pummel them, but the memories didn't bother him as much as they probably should have. For once in his life, he felt like he could just shrug it off.

You don't belong here anymore. You don't belong here anymore. He'd remembered he'd started repeating that single phrase over and over again, when he was called back to the chalice before, but the anxiousness he felt before was replaced with cold, numbness.

There were three yellow sofas decorating each side of the wall. Everything on the interior was different shades of yellow and gold. He spun his braid in a circle, for some reason it was comforting.

There was a desk right across from the door where a girl in a lily green dress with her honey-colored hair in a braid was sitting.

Ryker took out the note that he was keeping in his coat pocket and placed it on the desk in front of her.

Without looking up from her paperwork she shrugged. "You know the drill, weapons on my desk because she doesn't respect my need to keep my desk clear of non-essential documents."

KiKi was an old friend, she was one of Helga's favorite tools along with Ryker. "A pretty woman greeting them at the door will always draw in the rich men." As Helga put it.

KiKi used to give certain kids extra helpings at lunch, Ryker was one of them.

Ryker started pulling out his knives. Two in each sleeve, four in each side of his jacket, one in each boot, two strapped to both of his thighs by leather belts, and four more strapped to his belt. He had twenty-two knives on him all day. It used to be uncomfortable, but he'd grown used to it.

KiKi looked up at him then nodded towards a door off to the left. "She isn't the happiest, so good luck." With a nod Ryker started for the door. "Ryker, please be careful." KiKi called after him.

"Uh-huh." Ryker replied, waving her off as he entered the room.

It was Helga's office, a desk in the middle of the room that Helga was reading a book at, with six largely built men posted in the room, two at the door, two beside the desk and two in the back corner of the room. Hanging on the wall above her was the cane of punishment, the sight of it was chilling.

Without his knives Ryker felt completely defenseless. He did know hand to hand combat, but the guards were twice the size of him plus he was wildly outnumbered. He walked over to her desk and Helga smiled when she noticed him.

"Sit." She said, motioning toward one of the chairs in front of her desk.

"I'd rather stand." He grumbled. "Now what do you want?" She looked at one of the guards at the door. He walked over and grabbed Ryker by the shoulders and pushed him into the seat. The guard let him go but stayed right behind him.

"I see you still have people wrapped around your finger." Ryker rubbed one of his shoulders. She shrugged

"Onto business, there is a rather troublesome pub owner, who is making threats against one of our clients. He's paid handsomely, I just need you to break into his house and leave this note. It's a very simple mission." Helga told him, placing a small piece of parchment on the table in front of him.

"So why can't one of your other pets do it?" Ryker hissed, stuffing the note into his pocket.

"Because you're going to leave me soon and I want to use you whilst I still can. Plus, it's fun to torment you. Now unless you want the price that Dustmark must pay to go up a couple thousand gold pieces, take the note, and get it done. Now get out." Ryker glanced behind him; the other goon was approaching.

"Hang on, that's all I have to go on? Where even is this guy?" The guards grabbed Ryker's arms and lifted him up off the chair.

"You're losing your touch, Ryker." Helga looked back down at the book she was reading earlier.

"What is that supposed to mean?" Ryker snarled as he struggled against the guard's iron grip. One of the guards punched Ryker across the face, bringing stars to his eyes.

They dragged Ryker past KiKi, and he shrieked as they tossed him out onto the dirt street. He landed hard on his side. Rolling onto his back, he closed his eyes, and groaned as he heard chuckles from the bystanders. *That hurt.*

"You just can't stay out of trouble, can you?" He heard KiKi giggle above him. His eyes snapped open. She stood above him with a medium sized sack over her shoulder. Ryker sat up as she dropped it into his lap and walked back into the chalice shaking her head. *Well at least she gave me my knives back.*

Chapter 9

Ryker

The sun had just started rising when Ryker was walking up to

the porch of the Red Wyvern. He noticed two odd men standing near

the entrance, it wasn't the normal doormen.

He made it into the tavern with only a glower from each of them, which wasn't odd.

He weaved his way through the kitchen and got a couple of odd glances which weren't exactly normal. After making his way to the back room he held up his dragon pendant, muttered the incantation and the green outline appeared. While ascending he heard indistinct talking.

"Eric, there are some weird guys at the door, did you want me to-" Ryker paused his sentence at the sight of a third guy in the room. Whose eyes narrowed the second they laid on Ryker.

"A part-elf?" He demanded. Eric, who hadn't given either of them a thought until now, glanced up, his eyes widened when he saw Ryker. He noticed Gilbert was staring at him too.

"What happened to your face?" Gilbert went face to face with him.

"You mean other than the fact that he's a part elf?" The other man in the room growled. Eric walked over to him, and they started talking quietly so Ryker or Gilbert couldn't hear, but he saw a hint of anger in Eric's eyes.

"What are you talking about?" Ryker distanced himself a little.

"Um, did you not notice the giant mark on the left side of your face? What happened?" Ryker walked over to a mirror that hung on the wall. There *was* a giant red mark on the side of his face where the guard had hit him. Gilbert poked at it.

"Stop it! What are you? Five?" Ryker snapped, slapping his hand away. Gilbert threw his hands up.

"Yeah, five heads taller than you."

"Excuse me?"

Eric cleared his throat.

"Ryker, this is Arloon Musiak. Now we need to explain business. Do you have the book?" Ryker fished out the book and put it on the desk.

"Told you." Gilbert said smugly to Arloon.

Eric and Arloon chattered back and forth at one another. Talking about business, nothing Ryker cared much about.

Ryker reached to start fiddling with his watch, but when he felt it, he immediately felt that it was smashed to pieces. His heart dropped. *They must've broken it when they threw me out.*

His thoughts drifted to his father, and he remembered the last words he'd spoken to him. *No matter how you see this in the future, remember, we had no choice, this watch is a reminder that our love will be with you even when we are not.*

He hadn't known what his father meant then, but he did now. *Certainly, they loved me, even though they sold me.* But if that was true, why didn't they have a choice? Why did they choose to leave him if they apparently loved him? Wouldn't they have found another way?

He didn't know much about his mother other than she was an elf so she couldn't come to Hadune, he often caught himself wondering if she'd been hunted down.

Ryker's hand went to his braid again. He wanted to twirl it, but that would probably be rude. He settled for rubbing the plaits in between his fingers and focusing on his happy memories.

He remembered they used to live on the road and slept in a wagon, he had a few vague memories of his parents' voices and wisdom, but he couldn't remember what either of them looked like.

Gilbert nudged him, bringing him out of his thoughts and back into the present.

"Well, I suppose now is a good time for a confession." Arloon took a step away from the table. "There is no mention of dragons in that book."

"What?!" All three of them demanded at once. Arloon threw his hands up. "I can explain. I needed to know you were committed."

"I'm sorry, you what now?" Ryker growled.

"You had us risk our necks for a loyalty test?!" Gilbert was glaring at him, and Eric had his arms folded over his chest.

"Now, now, let's not get angry. Now that I know you're committed I'll have my men send you information soon enough. I merely need a few hours or so to mull things over." Arloon made his way back toward the stairwell.

"I'll show him out." Gilbert grumbled before following him. After they were gone Ryker stuffed his knife back and looked at Eric.

"I cannot be the only one confused right now." Eric shook his head and thumbed through the tome's pages. "Well, I'm sure Gilbert is also confused. Where'd you get the bruise?" Ryker shifted.

He didn't like telling people about his dealings with Helga, he didn't want to explain himself to anyone, and even though Gilbert and Eric already knew that was where he was raised, they didn't know he was still summoned from time to time.

"Unrelated, can you fix this?" Ryker pulled the pieces of his watch and placed them on the desk beside the book. Eric's brow furrowed as he picked up the pieces.

"Would this happen to be affiliated to the bruise?" Ryker was going to lie and say he crushed it on the mission, but to Ryker's luck Gilbert came back up the stairs, cutting off the conversation.

"Is anyone else as confused as I am?" Ryker nodded and glanced back at Eric.

"It's rather simple really. He didn't know if he could trust us, so he sent us on a fool's errand." Eric was trying to figure out how to fix the watch. "And what in the world happened to this thing?" Ryker walked over and picked up the front covering. "Like I said, long story."

Chapter 10

Gilbert paced around the office while Eric sat at his desk still attempting to fix Rykers watch. He could hear the bustling of opening time downstairs. Ryker had turned into bed an hour ago and Gilbert had been debating following him, but it seemed like Ryker wanted to be alone. Seeing as they shared a room Gilbert didn't want to invade.

"What do you make of everything?" Asked Gilbert, finally breaking the silence.

"It's just casual business. He trusts us now and that's all that matters." Eric replied. *Does he ever stop thinking about himself and his money?* Gilbert leaned on the desk and eyed the pieces of the watch.

"I meant about Ryker."

"If he wanted to tell us he would."

"Unless he doesn't trust us."

"If he doesn't trust us, we cannot perform effectively as a team, and I'd have to send him back." Gilbert opened and closed his mouth a few times before he finally threw his hands up in frustration and stormed off. *How could he even think about sending him back!?*

He stomped through the kitchen to the stairs and to his and Ryker's room. Silently he opened the door.

The room was rather small with two cots and white sheets. They each had a trunk at the end of their cots, and there was a coat rack by the door, Ryker's coat hung there. There was one window between each of the cots, the blinds were closed so the light didn't flood through as they normally did.

Ryker was curled into a protective ball with his hands covering his head, he'd explained it was a habit he'd acquired at The Chalice.

"It was the safest way to sleep seeing as you didn't know who was going to get you up." He'd explained. "If it was Helga, you'd get a bang on the door, if it was one of her goons you'd get yanked out of bed by your hair."

His hair, which was usually in a loose braid, was tied into a loose, low ponytail. His blankets looked as if he'd fallen asleep under them but had ended up crawling out of them.

His knives were laid on the top of the trunk along with his belts and some odd black leather knife sheaths that looked like bracelets. According to Ryker he slid them on underneath his sleeve so that when he was pulling his knives from his sleeves, he wouldn't cut himself. His shoes were sitting in front of the trunk.

Gilbert sighed. He'd walked over and pulled the covers back over Ryker's shoulders when he noticed Ryker had a knife in hand. Gilbert gently slid the knife out of his grip. Ryker was seemingly always tense, even in his sleep.

Gilbert put the knife in with the others then sat down on his own cot. He slipped off his jacket, vest, and shoes.

He leaned against the wall and thought about his parents.

His father was a general of the legion, which was the army during the crown wars and now it was the city watch.

His father was the one to teach him how to shoot, how to ride a horse, how to drive a carriage, his father taught him nearly everything he knew. *Always expect the unexpected.* He'd told him. Gilbert got his compassion and his humor from his mother.

Promise me that you'll always look out for those who have nothing. That you'll be there for those who have no one. Her voice rang through his head as he glimpsed Ryker.

Ryker didn't have anything or anyone before he met Gilbert. He remembered the first time he'd met Ryker.

He seemed distressed and rather terrified of everything; he hadn't even said a word to Gilbert until probably two weeks after they met. He was even timid about anyone touching him, which to Gilbert was astonishing.

Gilbert recalled the first time he tried to give Ryker a high-five, he ended up flinching then looking confused when nothing happened. When Gilbert tried to explain what he was doing Ryker just looked embarrassed and vanished. It took a while, but Gilbert had gained his trust.

He was just relieved that Ryker now had Gilbert to watch over him. *Perhaps Mama would be proud.* His mother used to work at an orphanage, she'd said the sad stories of the children had always broken her heart. Gilbert had befriended plenty of children there when he was younger. If anything, he enjoyed watching out for people like Ryker.

After a while the door creaked open and Eric strolled in with Rykers watch in hand. It was put properly back together. He set it down next to his knives. He stared down at them for a moment.

Eric started rearranging his knives, he could tell they were by length. He spent perhaps five minutes merely moving them around, before he started straightening other things.

That was Eric, everything had a specific place, he would make sure everything was organized and everything was neat. He'd often obsess over something that was even an inch crooked, sometimes to the point of anger. It was the reason Ryker and Gilbert weren't allowed in his office much.

"You can calm down, no one's going anywhere." Eric said as he started folding Ryker's jacket and putting it beside the knives on the trunk. Gilbert sat up and crossed his arms. "I apologize, I spoke out of turn. It's been a long night."

"I wouldn't say it's me you should be apologizing to." Eric glanced at Ryker and rolled his eyes.

"I'm sorry." He whispered. "Happy?"

"I suppose so."

Eric shook his head and grabbed Gilbert's tailcoat, which was draped over the end of the bed, and started folding it. Gilbert didn't mention anything, Eric would just deny his obsession and claim that Gilbert and Ryker were just a disaster.

He set the now folded coat on Gilbert's trunk, only to start folding his vest, which was thrown over the side of the trunk.

"Get him up in an hour, I'm finishing up the plan." Eric ordered after straightening Gilbert's shoes and headed for the door.

"Oh, come on, we've been up all night with hardly any sleep the night before, can't we have a little more time? And aren't we supposed to know where we're going? Aren't we supposed to wait for his men to return?"

"Well, perhaps you shouldn't have been wasting your time at rival taverns last night. Either way, don't concern yourself with the details of business, just do as I say. As for rest, you can sleep when we're rich, I repeat one hour." Eric trudged out of the room and slammed the door shut.

How is he not tired? Ryker rolled over with a groan. Probably waking up to the loud *Thud!* of the door.

Gilbert laid back down and interlocked his fingers behind his head. Before he knew it, he was fast asleep

Chapter 11

Eric

Gilbert was still asleep. Eric sat alone in his office, facing his

grandfather's portrait. He couldn't help but feel empty staring at it.

He missed him. His father was always busy with the business, and his mother was busy soaking up the fame, so his grandparents practically raised him and his brother. His grandfather taught him to ride, taught him about magic, pretty much everything there was to know about how to run a business, and how to fix a wagon wheel.

His grandmother taught him to sew, to cook, and how to wash clothes. Even with all their servants, she always told him "If you want something done right, do it yourself." Eric used to live by that, but ever since he met Gilbert, he started to rely on him far more than he would've liked. Same went for Ryker.

His father, on the other hand, always told him the servants were there for a reason. He was raised that the help was the help. They were common people; they didn't have feelings. His grandparents told him otherwise.

After a while of quiet Eric called out.

"Ryker, is there something you want to tell me?" Eric felt the shift in the room a few minutes ago when Ryker entered through the window, which means he wanted Eric to know he was there. If Eric had to guess, he was sitting in the rafters.

There was a soft *Thump* behind him and the ruffle of papers. He spun his chair around. Ryker was sitting on Eric's desk, chin resting on his knees.

"Perhaps." He wasn't wearing his jacket anymore, and his ankle-length hair was tied into a high ponytail by a golden clip.

Eric crossed one leg over the other and folded his arms across his chest, forcing himself not to get up and gather the papers that were now strewn on the floor.

They sat in silence for a while. If Ryker wanted to share, he would. He just needed some patience.

He'd always taken his time when it came to telling someone anything. Trust was a fragile thing, especially with Ryker.

Ryker pulled some folded paper out of his jeans' pocket and handed it to him. Eric knew exactly what it was as soon as he unfolded the paper. A chalice summons.

"I see. What'd she want?"

"She wanted me to leave a note in some pub owner's house, but all she gave me was this." He handed him another piece of paper.

It had the insignia of the green flail with a red slash through it.

"I'm tired of being her toy." Ryker complained as he crossed his legs like Eric had and started playing with one of the desk toys.

"Hmm." Eric replied, noncommittally, fighting the urge to snatch the desk toy out of his hands.

He didn't like it when people touched his things, especially when they didn't put it back exactly where it was, but he knew that Ryker fidgeted with things to calm his nerves, so Eric had a feeling Ryker couldn't help it.

He knew the owner of the Green Flail. He knew where he lived, and probably could give Ryker a plan to get in and get out easily, but if Ryker didn't want to help Helga, Eric wasn't going to make him.

"I'll take care of it. How about you go find Gilbert? I still have some things around here that need doing before we leave tomorrow; you can go and enjoy yourself for a while." Eric handed both papers back to him.

"Am I to know where we're going, or should I just leave that to you?" Ryker asked as he slid off the desk and started to gather the papers he'd strewn on the floor.

"Awh, Ryker, you give me such relief on these things. If only Gilbert could be as trusting as you. Just leave all the details to me." Eric replied, fixing the desk toy back to where he had it before.

With a faint smile and a quiet nod Ryker climbed out the window. Eric lost sight of him when he closed it again. Part of Eric wanted to know how he did that, but some things just took a certain person's touch.

Eric started going through the papers and organizing them by order of importance.

He wished Gilbert would be more like Ryker in some ways. Ryker didn't need to ask a million questions, all he asked was 'What do I do?'. Of course, that's probably a habit of the chalice.

Eric didn't mind questions so much; it was the nagging that got him. Gilbert would whine like a child anytime he didn't know something. Ryker also didn't test Eric's limits as much as Gilbert.

Eric tried to keep his emotions out of business, and that was what his relationship was with both Gilbert and Ryker, business. However, when it came to those two, his emotions always managed to sneak in.

Now, he didn't need that happening. If he was going to pay for Ryker, he needed this job to go perfectly. There was no room for emotions or mishaps. No matter how that looked to anyone else.

Eric set the papers back down to where they were before Ryker had strewn them everywhere. *Keep your focus on the job, no distractions*

Chapter 12

The company rode on horseback, heading north to Pastow. It was either a large village or a small city. Eric knew where to go but he decided it was best Ryker and Gilbert didn't know, lest they got captured, or double-cross him.

Arloon had pointed out there were many rival gangs and powerful men after the same thing they were, he thought it best they didn't know that either.

It was well known that the search for the dragon eggs had been ongoing for years. The minute anyone hears about any kind of sign that someone may know something it will lead directly to The Fangs.

They were a few days into their trip and were only a few leagues away from Pastow and Gilbert and Ryker had hardly spoken a word to Eric. He was pretty sure Gilbert had told Ryker a couple days ago what Eric said about sending him back as he'd noticed Ryker had gone silent that night. He often did that when Eric and Gilbert would argue and there was yelling involved. He would also go quiet if there were too many people in one room.

He didn't care, Ryker needed to trust Eric, Eric didn't see the need to trust Ryker as he still wasn't fully certain of his loyalties.

"How much longer?" Gilbert called from behind him.

"Two leagues." Eric focused back on the forest beside the trail they were on. Huge trees and bright green grass, birds chirping, and squirrels running through the trees.

He glanced back at Gilbert and Ryker. Gilbert was looking at the forest with his fingers drumming the handle of one of his crossbows, he was evidently tense, which wasn't like him.

Ryker, on the other hand, never looked more at home, he fit rather well in the forest, as most elves did. As far as Eric knew, he hadn't been outside of Hadune since he was eight and Eric could see his excitement and the gleam in his eyes with every moment away from Helga and away from all the glares from the people. *I better hope he doesn't get attached; I can't afford a new ghost. Well, I suppose after this job I could.*

"So, you've been rather secretive." Said Gilbert as he rode next to Eric.

"You haven't been talking much either, Pridestone."

"Oh, you *are* angry with us."

"I'm not angry, I'm just focusing on the mission, not laughing with the elf." As much as Eric liked Ryker, he wouldn't admit it. Especially with Gilbert. He was a very sentimental person.

"So, he's just an elf now?"

"Isn't that what he is?" Gilbert scoffed and drifted back beside Ryker, who was staring at the colorful butterfly that had landed on his finger. *Better they be agitated at me than be asking questions.*

Eric

A few hours later Pastow came into view. It was a lively place, and no one gave them a second thought as they passed through the street with horses in tow. After they found and paid a stable boy to take care of the horses, they found an inn.

Arloon had given them plenty of money to get them housing and food. The only one who was disappointed with the lodgings was Ryker, who evidently preferred the camping that they'd been doing, and much more enjoyed being outside in the forest.

The room had two beds with pale yellow sheets, two windows on each wall with yellow curtains pinned to the wall to let the sunshine flow in creating a warm ambiance to the room. Nightstands and dressers decorated the wall which was patterned with gold leaves and vines.

"I could get used to this!" Gilbert announced plopping down on one of the beds.

"Mhm." Ryker mumbled. He shifted his bag from one hand to the other.

Thinking about it, Eric noticed the room reminded him of the Chalice. Ryker seemed to realize it too, his muscles were taut and with his free hand he started to twirl his braid in a circle. It was hard to tell whether his stress was from being out of Hadune for the first time in eleven years or being in a place that looked like the Chalice.

"You can have the bed, Eric." Ryker offered as he started to pick at his lip with his free hand. He dropped his bag down beside the door.

"I'm gonna explore the town, see what I can find." Gilbert jumped up off his bed with a smile and turned to Ryker. "Wanna come?" Ryker nodded. "Care to join us, Eric?"

Eric eased over to his bed and started straightening the pillows, he shifted the portraits and other decorations that were even slightly off center. *Who doesn't straighten the room before you leave it?* He thought angrily.

"I'll stay here and do some research; I could have sworn I saw a library down there."

Chapter 13

The room that Eric got was more than disturbing. It was

nearly an exact copy of the Chalice's main room.

Ryker hated how it made his skin crawl, but he couldn't help it. Part of him felt like Helga or one of her goons were going to pop out at any minute.

It didn't help that most of the people they passed towered over him, just like a goon would. He couldn't help but feel he was still in danger. *You're fine.* He told himself. *Gilbert's right here, Eric isn't far. You're being irrational.* He'd recited that too many times to count in his time away from the chalice, but there was always that fear in the back of his mind. Sometimes he felt it became so overwhelming he couldn't speak, especially when people yelled or even got mildly angry with him.

Although, it wasn't just how the room looked, Ryker had been to Pastow before, even though he decided to keep that from Eric and Gilbert.

Helga would take them to different towns and cities to perform, it helped pick up business to see what the assassins could do.

Aerial silks, tightropes, trapeze, the hoop, Ryker had done it all. He even dabbled in a bit of ballet, mainly for the discipline it taught, but he mostly stuck with acrobatics.

In the air was where Ryker felt most at home, it was like he was above the world's problems. Of course, he'd only traveled once before he was sold.

Most times he performed at taverns, inns, anywhere in Hadune they needed entertainment.

Ryker used to be a slave he practically still was. He'd been working for Eric for a year now and he still didn't know exactly what he'd gotten himself into. The only thing Eric promised was that he'd have more freedom with them than with Helga. He was right, but he was still a slave, he had a tattoo to prove that.

Every time someone is sold from the chalice, they get a tattoo to show who owns them, it was Helga's protection guarantee, it would lead enemies to the new owner, rather than her. Ryker had a black tattoo on his shoulder of a fang with wyvern wings.

That day at The Chalice all Ryker wanted was a way out, away from Helga, away from the constant beatings, and away from being anyone's puppet.

What Ryker didn't realize when he'd agreed was that he was still going to be a puppet. After he was sold his strings weren't cut like he'd hoped, only extended. Eric was still the puppet master and Ryker was still his puppet.

When he was at The Chalice, he was desperate for any chance at getting out and he took the first chance he got. *I was so stupid. If only we had spoken more and talked more about what I'd be doing, I could still be at The Chalice with my friends.*

He often caught himself longing for the Chalice, longing for Helga. She had a disgusting way of convincing the children that she was the only person to ever care for them. She manipulated them into believing that they had no place in the world unless they were with her, that no one would ever love them and that the beatings were from a place of love. In all honesty, Helga was the only mother he'd ever really known, and as evil as she was, he still often missed her. Sometimes he felt so lost without her.

Ryker didn't want to think about The Chalice, pretty much ever again. He turned his focus on the bustling street and Gilbert who was clutching Ryker's arm and leading him in front of plenty of booths selling different things. There was some cheese, some seasonings, and some fancy festival masks. Nothing that piqued Rykers interest, but Gilbert tried everything

"You think I would look good as a jackal?" Gilbert asked, putting it over his face, but it wasn't fully on.

"Well, it is an improvement." Gilbert looked hurt.

"Unnecessary."

Their conversation was cut off by yelling and shrieks down the road. Ryker and Gilbert locked eyes. With a nod Gilbert took off toward the shrieks and Ryker weaved through the chaos in the crowd and scaled the wall of a house.

Once he made it to the roof, he could see what was going on. A group of people were surrounded by a ring of fire. Soldiers howled for water, people were screaming, and some odd bald men came from the shadows and started dispatching the soldiers.

Ryker pulled his hood and mask up and leapt from rooftop to rooftop, not slipping once.

"Kill them!" He heard the soldier's yell. He saw a small crossbow bolt tear through one. Gilbert fired another, only nicking one of the other bald men.

Ryker pulled his knives from his sleeves, his favorite type of knife. They were like brass knuckles that had a button to release a hidden small blade.

His knuckles may have been his favorite, but he loved all his knives. They were thin, easy to throw. He'd even named a few of them. Sitari on his hip, Zealous on his left thigh, Vindicator in his left coat sheath and Nyxus in the right one.

Nyxus meant moon, Sitari meant star in elven. The elves believed that the sun and moon were brothers, working in harmony to protect the realm. Most elves believed the moon watched over them as at night no humans hunted.

Ryker had always loved the way the moon shone above the chaos of Hadune, it had always granted him the only peace he could find.

He jumped off the roof and landed gingerly behind one of the bald men. Ryker slit his throat and pounced on one of the other ones, ramming his knife in the back of his neck.

When Ryker looked up from the now dead man's body, he saw one of the soldiers staring at him with wide eyes. He looked around Rykers age, but he had a slight beard.

"Sorry!" Ryker announced kicking him in the face, knocking him out cold. *Hopefully he won't remember me.* Gilbert may not have minded openly helping the soldiers, but Ryker preferred not to be seen.

None of the other soldiers seemed to notice Ryker, so he did what he did best: disappear.

He glided back into the alleyway and watched the soldiers finish off any other bald men, but he didn't see Gilbert. He closed his blades and shoved them back into his sleeves. He pulled his mask and hood down.

Ryker slid into a crowd of people who moved away from the chaos. Once he broke away and eased through the streets looking for some sign of Gilbert when he heard groaning.

Ryker followed the sound to find Gilbert leaning on the wall beside the porch of a tavern with his hand on his bleeding thigh.

Ryker knelt down and helped put pressure on his thigh. Gilbert sucked in sharply.

"What happened?"

"I got stabbed by a unicorn. What do you think!?" Gilbert snarled.

"No need to get snippy. Come on, let's go find Eric."

Chapter 14

Ryker

Gilbert sat on a crate in the alleyway next to the inn.

They didn't want to draw attention to themselves, so they tucked themselves away.

"What were you two thinking?!" Eric stood near them; arms folded over his chest. He reminded Ryker of Helga, scolding them for every little thing.

He could feel himself starting to sweat. *No, Eric isn't Helga, I'm fine.*

He often felt like he was sweating more than he should be when his mind would start to race. Assuring himself it was just Eric, and he was safe, helped with things like that. Gilbert being there was helpful too, as he knew Gilbert wouldn't let Eric hurt him. *Focus on what you're doing.*

Ryker had bound Gilbert's leg with his scarf to help keep the bleeding under control, but it was a deep gash and it needed medical attention Ryker couldn't give.

He kept his eyes on Gilbert's leg, not really wanting to make eye contact with Eric. He wanted to answer Eric's question, he wanted to speak and explain himself, but his lips remained sealed. *I don't even know what I was thinking. Do what Gilbert does, perhaps? Why does it seem like I can never talk when it's important? This is getting old.*

"I'm hoping that this doesn't stain my scarf." Gilbert winced as Ryker pulled the scarf tighter.

"He needs a healer." Ryker murmured. He wanted to say more, but he physically couldn't bring himself to. Eric scoffed.

At The Chalice they had to learn to patch themselves up. They were given supplies, but no instructions. So, Ryker only knew how to treat minor cuts and sprained or broken bones.

"I know someone, but she won't be happy. Stay with him until I return. This is coming out of your pay, Gilbert." Eric stormed off into the crowded streets, leaving Ryker and Gilbert alone in the alley.

With Eric gone Ryker could feel himself relaxing.

Ryker trusted Eric, as much as someone like him could, but his anger wasn't the easiest thing to deal with. It became overwhelming very quickly. Whether it was a reflex, or a fear Ryker couldn't tell, but it often rendered him speechless, which granted Ryker some frustration when he couldn't form words no matter how hard he wanted to.

Ryker stood up and leaned against the wall across from Gilbert, keeping his eyes on the streets.

He wanted nothing more than to go back into the forest. He hadn't felt that free since he was sold.

Gilbert thought that Eric allowed him enough freedom, but he was stuck going wherever Eric went, doing whatever *Eric* wanted. It may not have been the chalice, but being bought by Eric was a different type of prison. Even more miserable at times when freedom was just within his grasp, yet it seemed to constantly slip through his fingers. *I could just go now. Make it to Llonderell and try to find my parents.*

Llonderell was an impenetrable haven for elves. It was the only haven for elves. It was founded hundreds of years ago by some elven chief.

He remembered how his mother told him stories about the giant white castle built into the side of a mountain with the huge halls and ballrooms. Apparently, that was where Ryker was born, but they had to flee due to an attack that they blamed his father for.

He looked at the ailing Gilbert. *He wouldn't be able to stop me.*

He could've left, but Eric and Gilbert were his friends, the only people he could trust. He couldn't just leave them. Especially since neither of them had any medical experience. *Eric is getting a healer though. Then they wouldn't need me.* Ryker's hand went to Nyxus' handle, it was cool to the touch. It was calming, reassuring.

"How long do you think Eric's gonna be?" Gilbert asked, breaking Rykers train of thought. He shrugged. He felt like he could speak again, but part of him just didn't want to.

"Oh, please tell me you have a distraction."

"Um, okay. I'll find an object and you can ask yes or no questions to figure out what it is." Ryker offered

"So, a children's game?"

Ryker sighed. "Do you want a distraction or not?"

Chapter 15

Eric slid around the people in the crowded streets. He was

more annoyed than anything else. He wasn't surprised Gilbert got

involved, but Ryker should've known better. They needed to lay low,

they didn't need to cause a stir or draw attention to themselves.

Gilbert had assured him the legion was too busy to care that they were there, but Eric knew that the legion in smaller towns cared far more about the law than in Hadune.

The commotion from the attack was dying down now, so it made things easier to weave between the people.

Eric knew these streets like the back of his hand. Just after his parents kicked him out, he stayed in Pastow with a friend until he was back up on his feet. Unfortunately, it looked like it was time for another favor.

He found himself outside the infirmary. It wasn't as crowded as one might think. It seemed whoever caused the chaos of earlier didn't harm many people.

It was a smaller building, but it was far bigger than its neighbors. It was big for a house, small for a hospital. There were wooden steps that led up to the wooden door with two lanterns on either side of it. A stone foundation could be seen behind the steps.

He eased up the steps, running through what he would say. His old healer friend lived here. Adaline Neso. She used to be his grandfather's old nurse, they let her go a few months before he died.

As Eric spent most of his time near his grandfather, Adaline and Eric became quite close. She was the first person he went to after his parents kicked him to the curb.

He slipped in the door.

The room was filled with torches and chairs. It was quaint, just like how he remembered it. There was a desk in front of the wall that was between the two corridors.

A man, dressed just as fine as Eric was, sat at the desk. He had shaggy black hair and hazel eyes. He was the receptionist, Jake Reedi, he was a spoiled brat. His father owned the place and gave him a job, it was obvious he thought that papa giving him a job made him something.

"Well, well, I knew you wouldn't make it far in Hadune." He said as Eric approached. "Come to ask Adaline for a place to stay?"

"I am here to see Adaline, if you must know, but not for a place to stay. It's for a business opportunity." Eric said as he started straightening the papers, bottles, desk toys, pretty much anything that wasn't perfect, Eric fixed.

"Well, lucky for you she is finishing up her last appointment for the day. Of course, you being Mister business now, I would understand if you had a meeting with your associates." Jake mocked. Eric didn't know if he knew about his tavern or if he was just being Jake. "I can always tell her why you came to see her. Eric wants to know if you wanted to lose all your money on a dead-end business venture. Oh, what's that? You don't? Well, I'll let him know." Jake chuckled.

"Thank you for your input, Jake. I'll see myself in." Eric replied as he walked past the desk to the corridor on the right.

Eric couldn't help but feel that same old frustration he'd had before. Why was the frustration he had when he was younger resurfacing? He thought he had gotten a handle on it, until Jake had to open his giant mouth. His jaw clenched as his mocking set in. *Just wait until I become richer than his and my family combined.*

He eased through the hall until he saw Adaline waving an old woman goodbye. Her eyes widened when she saw Eric.

The old woman smiled as she passed him. "You know, my husband has a cane like that."

Eric smiled and nodded in reply. That was the real difference between Pastow and Hadune. The people would exchange pleasantries, even if they didn't know each other. In Hadune, if you tried to do that, you'd probably lose your wallet.

Adaline grabbed his wrist and pulled him into her exam room. She was wearing a simple, dark red gown, and her wavy, dark brown hair was pulled up into a bun. Her tan skin matched well with her ocean, upturned eyes and puffy pink lips.

"Eric? Why are you here? How'd it go in Hadune? Well, I would think it went pretty well seeing how you're dressed." Adaline rubbed her eyes. "Yep, it's you. I feel like the outfit could use a hat."

Eric was relieved she was still a chatterbox, and the fact that she judged his fashion sense, just like she used to. It was good to see her, so long she didn't know it was. He fixed his sleeves, which she'd ruffled when she grabbed him.

"I did have a hat once. I gave it to a friend, and I haven't gotten around to getting a new one." Eric grinned.

"You have a friend? I think I need to sit down."

"The one I'm mentioning is somewhere between friend and investment." She flashed a few teeth at that.

"That makes more sense for you."

"Well, I have a proposal. I think I should lead with saying that it would both get you away from the Reedi's and give you enough gold to buy a mansion."

"I don't need to hear anymore, I'm in. Just let me change."

Ryker

They'd played the game for about a half an hour before Eric returned with a woman in tow.

She had piles of wavy, dark brown hair with blue eyes. She wore a pink dress that went just above her knee decorated with dark red hearts and a hood. She had black leggings underneath and a bag that matched the tan of her boots, which went just below her knee.

"This is Adaline. The healer I told you about." Eric seemed calmer now, allowing Ryker to ease a little.

"Hi, nice to meet you." She curtsied.

Healers were rare, as were most mages these days. Most sorcerers focused for years on one kind of magic and very little focused on healing.

There were four different types of magic. Healing magic, destruction magic, elemental magic and creation magic. Most human mages after they discover their gift focus on either healing or elemental, as elves created destruction magic and creation magic and elves were seen as evil.

The only exception that Ryker knew was Eric, who practiced creation magic.

She knelt down next to Gilbert, untied the scarf around his thigh and handed it to Ryker.

"Gosh, I hope that didn't stain." Gilbert groaned. Ryker rolled his eyes.

Adaline dug through her bag and pulled out a jar of odd green salts. She popped off the cork and sprinkled some on the open gash in his leg. She waved her hands over the wound and watched it visibly close.

"Eric tells me you need a healer for a job. I'm all in."

Chapter 16

Back in the room, Gilbert was tasked with telling Adaline about the job and the fangs. Eric had gone back to the library and Ryker had disappeared as he usually did. Gilbert was sitting on his bed and Adaline was sitting on Eric's.

"So, you, a sharpshooter, Ryker, a slave assassin, and Eric, a creation mage, are looking for a dragon egg?" She asked "Doesn't that seem a bit.... impossible?"

"Yes, but I have a question for you. What was going on with the fire and the bald men?"

"Oh, that. That's some elemental acolytes from the cult of Surach, god of chaos. The guards have been trying to stamp out the remains, but they keep popping back up. You'll find them pretty much wherever you go, it's honestly ridiculous."

"So, they kill people for fun?"

"No, for sacrifices. Anyway, back to my question. Why are you chasing fairytales?"

"Because it's huge money, and it's necessary. We need the money to free Ryker. Plus, I need a bed like this." Gilbert sprawled out. His cot at the wyvern wasn't nearly as roomy nor as comfortable as this.

"Free? You mean, buy, right?" Gilbert popped his head up.

"What?"

"You said 'free', but there won't be any real freedom involved. Sure, he isn't owned by Helga anymore, but he would still be owned by Eric. So, he isn't technically free." Gilbert sat up.

"But we don't consider *owning* him per se, more like saving him. I mean, unlike when he was with Helga, he can do what he wants."

"Except leave. He can do whatever he wants, as long as he has the time to do whatever *Eric* wants. Do you consider that free, Gilbert?" Gilbert's temper rose. *She's so condescending! She doesn't even know Ryker, yet she pretends to know everything!*

"Why would he *want* to leave?"

"Because he's tired of being owned by someone, he wants to find his family, he actually hates you, the list goes on. Why would he want to stay? It feels like you've been thinking of leaving as well, so why have *you* stayed?" Gilbert stood up and stormed off to go find Eric.

The thing that got him was that she was right. Why would Ryker want to stay? Why had Gilbert stayed so long? Was it because he felt obligated to help Eric, seeing as he put a roof over his head and kept him alive since he was sixteen? Was it because he thought he would get the riches that Eric promised? What was the point?

Gilbert strolled through the library, which was huge for the inn they were staying in.

It had about a dozen book shelves that lined the walls with polished wood and shiny floors with spotless rugs. Tables, chairs and desks were everywhere. Plenty of different people were searching and picking through the selection of books.

Eric was flipping through a book at a desk near the back.

"I can't stand her! She's so snobby, she thinks she knows everything about everyone!" He whispered harshly as he took a seat next to Eric.

"Don't *you*?"

"No! Well, maybe a little, but at least I actually know the person I'm talking about!"

"Well, get used to her, because Ryker doesn't know as much as I thought he did." Gilbert crossed his arms. *It's like he doesn't value my opinion! He's so self-righteous. Why* do *I stick with him?*

Gilbert waited around with Eric for about an hour until Adaline joined them.

"So, do you have any idea where we're going? Gilbert here didn't seem to know." Eric hadn't looked at either of them before, but now he looked up.

"Gilbert, where's Ryker?" Gilbert glanced at Adaline who looked just as confused. It was obvious Eric was dodging the question.

"Uh, no. You aren't getting out of this. Do you know where you're going, or are we just wandering aimlessly from town to town?"

"I know where we're going, you don't need to, the only way you're getting that money is with me. So just do what I tell you and don't ask questions."

"Oh no, you don't get to order me around. You don't own me." Adaline hissed. "You need me, and I need to know what I'm getting into." Eric sighed.

"I can't tell you where we're going, but I will explain more of *how* I know what I know."

Chapter 17

Adaline decided to spend most of the night with Eric and his crew. They were gathered in the inn's room, Ryker was sitting cross legged on one of the dressers, Eric was standing between the beds, Gilbert was sitting on his bed and Adaline sat on the floor.

It was midnight, so it was already dark out, Ryker had taken forever to return.

It was obvious Eric trusted her; she was the first person he went to after his father cut him off. Eric had explained what had happened and with their story, she couldn't just leave him. Which also was why she was in this job, not for the money, even though Eric promised her a share, she was in it to look out for Eric.

He had no one to help him after he was cut off, so it was good to see he had friends. But she still needed to make sure his 'friends' weren't going to go turncoat.

She'd gotten to know Gilbert and had a pretty good handle on him, he didn't seem like the backstabbing type. It was Ryker she was bothered by.

She'd tried to get Gilbert to give her reasons to trust Ryker, but when he stormed off, rather than jumping to his defense, it seemed she was correct in her suspicions. Ryker had no reason to stay or to be loyal to Eric other than Eric owning him.

She didn't want to talk to Eric about it without proper proof. She tried to focus on his body language and how he reacted to Eric's explanations, but there was something about him that made her forget that he was there.

She couldn't just stare otherwise he would know she was investigating him. He was silent, calculating, and a ruthless killer, that much she'd figured out. If there was something amiss about him, she'd figure that out too.

"So, Arloon gave you information that you can't tell anyone else, by his order?" Gilbert asked, obviously not believing him. Eric nodded. Gilbert went on complaining about how stupid it was and Eric just rolled his eyes.

Adaline turned her attention to Ryker; he was cleaning one of his knives. He didn't seem the least bit interested in what Eric had to say, other than a couple glances toward them, he seemed more interested in getting the dried blood off his knives. *I suppose if he was planning on leaving, he wouldn't care all that much.* She wanted to trust him, but he was making it difficult.

Ryker glanced back at her, and they locked eyes for a quick moment before she quickly looked back at Eric. She was conflicted, even though she knew he was a cold-blooded killer, there was still an innocent feel about him. *Don't let him fool you.* She told herself. *That's what he's trained to do. Elves are known for their deception.*

Gilbert was still complaining about not knowing any information. Part of Adaline wanted to complain as well, but if Eric was telling the truth, there was no point. She summoned her magic, all at once she could hear their heartbeats.

It was a special skill healers did to check up on their patients, but some could use it to find one single person, they just had to listen to it once.

Healers were workers of anatomy, some could control the blood in another's body, that was usually to stop bleeding, but sometimes they used to drop heart rates to make obnoxious patients pass out. Control of the blood was something out of Adaline's reach, but she could drop someone into a coma, it just took a minute.

Gilbert's heartbeat was normal, Ryker's was beating faster than it should, but then again, she'd never listened to an elven heartbeat before, Eric's on the other hand, was racing, he was lying. She didn't pry or point out that she could hear their heartbeats. She didn't want to show her cards before she was certain she could trust everyone. She relaxed, focusing on the actual conversation rather than their heartbeats.

She rubbed her ring. It was windcopper. Windcopper was a type of metal, it was also referred to as elf's bane. It would burn the skin off a full blood even if it was just brushed against one's skin. Most poachers used it as a threat to keep captured full bloods in check. She wasn't sure if it would work on a half-blood. She needed to test it

"Well perhaps, if you guys don't mind, I could sleep here tonight? Mainly because I quit my job, which is also where I lived, for this." *And to see what the elf gets up to after you go to sleep.* Gilbert shrugged.

"As long as you don't take my bed, I'm fine with it."

"You can have mine." Eric offered.

"I'll sleep on the floor, thank you. I need practice if I'm going to be traveling with you, won't I?"

"Suit yourself. We are leaving tomorrow night, but we are planning to do so don't think about sleeping in." Ryker stood up.

"I'll take to the streets, keep an eye out for the acolytes and such." *Sure, you will.*

She wanted to tell Eric about her suspicions, but without solid proof he could easily deny them. *Be patient.* She told herself Just *wait 'til they're asleep then sneak out after him and figure out what he's really doing.*

Chapter 18

Eric dreamt; He stood in front of Helga's desk tapping his

foot impatiently. Dressed in his usual suit, but with a hat.

He got information on other businesses propping up around Hadune and the lower ring. He paid an awful lot for the information and her silence. She had a lot of businessmen who rent or buy her spies or assassins and as they are loyal clients, she was reluctant to give any information that might jeopardize them and give her bad publicity.

He reached over and fixed the crooked desk statue; he'd been fighting the urge to do so for an hour now.

The door opened and in strolled Helga, her piles of copper hair in a bun with beads that decorated it. She wore a poofy, aqua blue, dress with creamy yellow accents and a plunging neckline, it dragged on the floor as she walked. She carried herself with an air of rectitude, even though she was a wretched woman with horrible morals.

She sat in her chair and looked up at him with a scathing frown.

"What do you want, street rat?" Eric smiled at her. "I don't have any new information, come back next week." Helga started signing documents. Eric scoffed and spun around. *All that waiting for nothing.*

There was no point in arguing. Helga was insufferable and wicked, but she wasn't a liar, at least not to her paying clients.

When he had made it outside and onto the street someone tapped him on the shoulder. He spun around. A young part elf boy, he couldn't have been older than eighteen, was standing behind him.

He was wearing one of Helga's spy garbs. A skintight black suit underneath a dark purple, flowy, silk shirt. A golden collar hung around his neck and a purple belt was around his waist. Golden earrings decorated the tips of his ears and a shiny golden headpiece with a purple gem dangling on his forehead. His silver hair was peeking out from underneath a vale attached to the headpiece. It seemed Helga had an expensive taste for her spies as well, but he was surprisingly thin. Dark purple spots had been painted up his neck and the side of his face, but he had four bright blue dots tattooed around his eyes and matching ear tips. He was so conspicuous. *How didn't I notice him?*

The spies and assassins that were trained in the chalice were taught to go unnoticed, but the paint and tattoos were odd, no other assassin had spots up their necks.

"Can I help you?" Eric asked as he dusted off his shoulder. The boy handed him a piece of paper. He opened it.

'The owner of the green flail is going bankrupt.'

He looked back up at the boy who was still standing there, silent as a ghost, but tugging at his shirt sleeve.

"Nobody gets something for nothing. What do you want?"

"Oi! Get back in here, you little imp!" Before the elf could even say anything one of Helga's bruisers was stomping over to them.

Before Eric could say that everything was fine, the boy snatched the note and hid it up his sleeve. The goon snatched the elf by the strange golden dog collar around his neck and yanked him backwards.

"Apologies on behalf of the chalice, this one slipped away." And with that he'd dragged the elf away.

The following week, Eric scraped up enough money to start payment on an assassin from the chalice.

"Well, we have many you can pick from Mister Dustmark. All of them are trained-" Eric held up a hand, cutting her off.

"I've seen them, and I know which one has the skills I need. I want a part elf. He had blue tattoos on his eyes and his ears." Helga's eyes had gone from annoyed to infuriated.

"That useless-Why on earth do you need Him?" Eric shrugged, he didn't need him, but he was still curious as to why he'd given him the note.

After a while haggling over his price, she finally gave in and sent for him. He'd entered with a fresh bruise on the side of his face.

Eric saw the fear in his eyes when he saw him.

"Well, you're his problem now, Ryker. Now, get out of my sight." The two of them walked out into the main room. Eric noted that his footsteps were silent, like a cat's.

"Do you have any items you need before we leave?" Ryker shook his head. "All right, I'll explain more once we arrive, until now," Eric put his own hat on Rykers head. "You run with me now, we'll have a lot of enemies, best not show your face until we can be sure where we stand. Now let's go get you some proper clothes."

Chapter 19

Ryker

Ryker was sitting on the roof of the inn, gazing out at the field of rooftops before him. He sat with his knees pulled into his chest, toying with his braid.

He'd grown to like it above the bustling chaos of towns and cities. The calm night air, the stars in the sky, the glowing moon, it all seemed so peaceful.

There wasn't usually so much peace in his life, not even in his sleep. While he was usually free to wander the streets, everyone seemed to glare at him, so he preferred to travel by roof to get what little semblance of peace he could.

When he was younger, he could sit on the rooftops of Hadune all he wanted, but in the end, he had a curfew, he eventually had to return to Helga.

Eric trusted him enough to return in his own time, so now he could spend more time away from home-base without the fear he had of Helga, but he was still a slave. He had essentially memorized the conversation they'd had when they'd returned to the wyvern.

"I'm warning you now, the last thing you'll find with me is freedom. However, I can promise you more freedom than you'll find with that monster Helga." Eric had said after Ryker had changed.

He hadn't said anything, though he wanted to. He had so many questions, but his tongue clung to the roof of his mouth.

Eric's brow furrowed. "Can you speak?" He had asked.

Ryker nodded, even though he was dying to say yes. Eric started to circle him.

"Go on then."

Ryker tried, but he felt the words get caught in his throat.

He'd expected to get smacked upside the head with Eric's cruel looking cane, but Eric had chuckled instead.

"Hm, well, I suppose you'll speak when you get comfortable here. For now, at least we know you can be quiet." Eric stopped in front of him. Ryker was annoyed with himself. He had a million words running through his mind, why couldn't he say just one? "Either way, you'll be doing similar things that you did in the chalice. Have you killed anyone before?"

Eric had reached over and started fixing Ryker's new jacket. He smoothed out wrinkles and straightened the sleeves.

Ryker shook his head no. He remembered freezing as Eric had touched him. It was one of those things that sent spiders up his spine.

Helga had assassins and spies, the only difference was what they specialized in and the work they were assigned.

Ryker had been good at everything, but she preferred to send Ryker spying on recon missions, seeing how he could seemingly melt into the shadows.

"Well, then you aren't opposed to the idea." Ryker *was* opposed to the idea, he'd wanted to say that, but the words got caught in his throat yet again. He'd let Eric think what he wanted; he'd learn to adjust.

In the lower ring of Hadune crime ran rampant, one more murder was nothing the legion cared about. Though it bothered him, he used it as cover, as protection.

If he was never caught and they didn't bother looking, then in a few days it was as if it never happened. Even now, thinking that twisted his stomach in knots. *When did I become so cruel?* He thought. *This was how you were raised. Don't blame yourself for your parents' mistake.* Another thought rang in his head.

Do you think farmers feel remorse after killing a cow for meat? No, because that's how they were raised. They were raised to know that was how the world works, they can't change how they were raised. Eric had explained after Ryker felt guilty about his first kill a few weeks later.

He wasn't a cow, Eric, and I'm not a farmer. Ryker had said defiantly. Eric had shaken his head.

No, you're a murderer in a city of thugs, thieves, and gangs. Now they'll know you aren't afraid to take a life. Use that as protection, stop denying what you are.

Ryker had stormed back to his room after that. He still kept the hat that Eric had given him, it was the first thing he'd officially been given. For some strange reason, it was comforting.

He pulled out the paper that Helga had given him before he left, it had nothing on it but a strange logo of a dark green flail with a red slash through it.

He hadn't had time to get to her mission. If he had to guess word had gotten back to her that he left without following her orders.

He knew Eric said he'd take care of it, but what if Eric didn't find time either?

He ran his fingers across the now fully formed bruise on the side of his face. He couldn't help but feel somewhat helpless. He had never failed to do a mission before. Even though he belonged to Eric, technically until the contract was fully paid off, she still had partial ownership. She could take it to a judge and have Ryker returned, seeing as time extensions that weren't in writing meant nothing.

With a sigh, he buried his face in his hands. Even though he hardly remembered them, he missed his parents. He kept telling himself they couldn't have known what Helga really did for a living, but what if they did? There always was that voice in the back of his mind telling him they knew; they just didn't care.

He wished he could see them. He didn't care if it was just for a minute. He had so many questions, but they all centered around the same thing. Why?

Why did they sell him? Why did they give him up? Why would they do that?

Someone grunted and squealed. He stiffened and whirled toward whoever it was, reaching for one of his knives on his belt.

Adaline was struggling to pull herself from the edge of the window to the roof.

He took a quick breath. *You're fine.* He thought, immediately annoyed at himself for getting startled so easily.

Ryker stood up, walked over and pulled her up by her wrists.

"Thank you." She smoothed her gown with her hands. "I've never really climbed anything before." She strolled back to where Ryker was sitting previously, stumbling in spots. Ryker chuckled.

"You aren't too shabby. I'd like to see Gilbert or Eric try to climb that. Either way, what brings you up here?"

"Just wondering where you were. You don't seem to stick around them much."

"Nah, Gilbert talks too much, and Eric brings down my mood with his perpetual brooding." Adaline laughed.

"Yeah, that sounds right. You come to the rooftops often?"

"Yup, it's much more... serene? I guess."

"Well, I suppose seeing as we're going to be spending time together, we might as well get to know each other." She extended her hand. Ryker clasped it. A fiery sizzle hissed against his skin, and he yanked it away. There was a bright red indentation on his hand.

"What's wrong?" Adaline asked. He looked at her hand. A silvery ring with a ruby red gem decorated her finger.

"Is that windcopper?" He asked.

Ryker had only encountered it once or twice, but he'd never been burned by it. Helga had made threats to use it on him before, but he knew better. She wouldn't threaten him with it if she actually had it. She would just use it.

"Yes." She answered. Ryker didn't like the gleam in her eyes. It was like a mad scientist just proved a hypothesis. He scooted away from her.

Now that he knew the ring was there, it was almost glowing in a way her other jewelry didn't. It was almost blinding. He'd seen windcopper before, it never glowed like that.

"I would appreciate it if you put it away." Ryker tried. "It's kind of hurting my eyes." She glanced down at it.

"Why? It isn't even touching you." she asked with a puzzled look on her face. He shrugged.

"Listen, I know what you're trying to do. You can trust me. Just please put that away." Ryker wanted to look away, but there was something so mesmerizing about it.

"It's my father's ring. He got it because he helped some poachers track down some full bloods. They burned our barn down. He gave it to me to protect myself. I don't like elves, and I'm not going to pretend to." Adaline stood up and walked back toward the window.

"Well, hang on. I didn't mean to offend you." Ryker called after her. "I take it back! You can keep the ring!" She climbed back down the side of the wall and presumably back through the window.

Now Ryker felt bad. He plopped back down with a sigh. *Well, that went well.* He rubbed the red indentation on his hand. *I Guess I need to wear my gloves more often if she's sticking around.*

Chapter 20

Eric

Eric and company were on the outskirts of Pastow. Night had fallen and they were preparing their horses. Eric's mind was elsewhere while he checked the harness on the saddle. They rested on his dream last night.

He often had dreams about the night he'd met Ryker. He wasn't sure why. He did notice there were always details missing. However, it did make it easier to compare the old Ryker to now.

He was far more confident. It was obvious to Eric the night they'd met he was underweight, so he'd filled out a little more. He'd been jumpy and anxious, but now he was more relaxed. He used to hate being touched and would flinch away, now he still didn't like it, but he was more amiable towards it. He only flinched if he was having a rough day.

Eric's dreams made it easier to see that he was more on edge than usual. If Eric had to guess it was thanks to Adaline.

Adaline naturally wasn't a very trusting person, and Ryker wasn't easy to trust when you first meet him, even Eric still had some doubts here and there. They were merely moments of weakness though; Ryker always found a way to pull through.

"We're ready to go." Gilbert called from behind him. He glanced backwards. Adaline was mounted on her horse beside Gilbert. Eric glanced at his packs. They were not organized; he must not have been paying proper attention to what he was doing while he was lost in his thoughts.

"Give me a few minutes." Eric replied as he started tightening the straps that connected them and arranging the smaller bags based on what they contained.

"You're only organizing things now? What have you *been* doing?" Gilbert asked.

"None of your business." Eric growled. Gilbert snapped his mouth shut.

A few minutes later, they were off. Eric led, Gilbert and Adaline were close behind, and Ryker had drifted behind them.

Ryker had been awfully quiet since last night. He was slightly worried Adaline said something. Elves allegedly had burned down her family's barn when she was younger, and she's hated them ever since. So, it wouldn't surprise him if Adaline didn't trust him.

They planned on riding through the night, so everyone had gotten up early and was tired. So, it wasn't like there was much talking anyway. Eric focused on the woodland around them.

The trail they were on had woodlands on either side of it, so it wasn't long before the tree branches stretched overhead, covering the moonlit sky. The patchy sky and stars were seen only in glimpses through the tree boughs. Tall, shadowed pines stretching up like arrows into the sky and glances of gray, puffy clouds against the inky night. It was all soothing, Eric always felt more attuned to nature at night.

Eric could hear the wind slipping through the leaves. Something cracking undergrowth with each step, the flutter of wings unseen, the horses' hooves snapping twigs as they trotted along, coyote calls, foxes yipping, and even some wolves howling in the distance. The sounds made it more eerie than it should've been.

"I'm not so sure I like this." He heard Gilbert whisper to Adaline.

"Me neither, it's very bizarre." She replied.

Eric agreed that it was creepy but traveling during the night avoided suspicion. Not that anyone in Pastow cared much, Eric wouldn't take any chances.

He glanced back behind him, Adaline and Gilbert still rode side by side, but Ryker wasn't riding behind them anymore.

Eric wanted to call for him, but he didn't bother. He could still sense him nearby, and Ryker hated it when people drew attention to him.

He rubbed the head of his cane. The silvery dragon reminded him of his grandfather, but it also had some actual use other than being an inconspicuous form of magic.

The connecting necklaces that the other fangs had were enchanted to track them. He didn't do it often, but it helped soothe his doubts. He didn't need to use it yet; he was positive Ryker was somewhere in the shadows. There certainly was plenty to hide in at this point.

On top of that, his cane was windcopper. He didn't tell anyone; he didn't see the need too. Windcopper looked a lot like silver, so it was hard to spot the difference. Either way, Ryker never touched his things and the cane hardly ever left Eric's side. On the off-chance Ryker did get burned Eric would probably have a lot of explaining to do.

"Eric."

He jumped at the sound of Ryker's voice beside him.

Ryker sat tall and splendid in his saddle, ankle-length braid running down his back and onto the horse's haunches. His dark blue cloak was pulled over both of his shoulders, not just thrown around one like usual. Even though tense, he looked completely at home. He was clearly not surprised that Eric jumped at his voice.

"What?" Eric smoothed some creases in his coat.

"You did remember to take care of that... thing with Helga, right?" He asked, almost as if Eric had forgotten.

"I told you not to worry about that." Eric eyed him.

He knew when it came to Helga, Ryker was quick to panic. He would usually just mess around with things, fidget with his watch, his braid, anything. At the moment he just sat staring at the road ahead, chewing on his bottom lip, which was new.

"I know, I just want to be sure I don't have to face her again."

Eric and Ryker sat quietly after that. He didn't know much about what Ryker faced with her, but he knew that Ryker couldn't go back.

Ryker's eyes rested on Eric's cane, and he squinted a little. Eric raised one Eyebrow at him. Ryker, clearly noticing Eric's expression, turned his attention back to the forest. *That was odd.*

"I just don't want to face her again." Ryker repeated, keeping his eyes on the trees.

Eric knew he shouldn't care as much as he did, but, against his better judgment, he had allowed himself to worry about Ryker. Gilbert and Adaline too.

"You won't have too. I took care of it." Eric didn't like how it sounded. He may have cared, but Ryker didn't need to know that. "Just focus on the job."

Chapter 21

They'd traveled all through the night and were still going

now. The sun had risen, allowing light to peek through the breaks in the

overhanging tree limbs.

The chirping of birds that replaced the hoots of owls warmed Adaline from the tips of her fingers to her toes.

Gilbert still rode beside her, they spoke on and off, but most of the time they stayed silent. She wasn't sure what Gilbert was paying attention to, but she was watching Eric and Ryker lead.

They'd gone farther ahead at some point in the night, but she could still hear them whispering back and forth at one another. What they were saying, she couldn't quite tell.

To be honest, she wasn't sure why she cared so much. She and Eric were close, yes, but close enough to warrant all this worrying? At least she knew that wasn't the only reason she was in this job, to show the Reedi's she was capable of more than looking at minor scrapes or taking care of obnoxious patients. She had the feeling Eric understood how she felt.

The Reedi's were one of the most respected families in Pastow, which made them overly entitled. They always denied Adaline the chance for a real career.

"So," Gilbert said. "Do you still hate Ryker?"

"Hate is a strong word." Adaline replied. No, it wasn't. That elf rubbed her the wrong way. Now that she knew her ring worked, she had some defense. She also knew Eric's cane was windcopper, meaning Eric wasn't totally defenseless against him either.

Although it was reassuring to see Ryker interact more with Eric. She knew Eric would never admit to it, but Ryker was someone he trusted, maybe even cared about. Adaline could tell by Eric's relaxed posture.

"I'm still a little unsure, but he seems nice enough." She said, lying again.

"Yeah, I felt the same way when I first met him. I'm gonna be honest." Gilbert nodded. "Eric assured me he was fine, but it did take a while. Just keep an open mind."

"Easier said than done." Adaline admitted.

"So, it is." He agreed.

Ryker slowed his horse until he was back next to Gilbert.

"Well, with all that being said, I'm going to talk to Eric." Gilbert urged his horse forward, leaving Adaline and Ryker by themselves.

She just eyed him.

"Adaline, about last night-" Ryker started, but Adaline cut him off.

"Save it." She snapped. His ears drooped. Part of her felt bad. "I understand that I can't blame you for what happened when I was a girl. I apologize." She sighed. There was one more thing she should probably apologize for as well. "And extending my hand just to see if my ring would work on you wasn't fair."

"Oh, no, it's okay. I'm used to people judging me because I'm an elf. It's all part of life." He eyed her ring. "I didn't know you did that just to see if it would burn me, though. That's a little harsh."

"It wasn't that harsh; it was a test." Adaline stated. "I don't plan on using it again."

"Promise?" Ryker asked. He glimpsed down at the hand she'd burned last night.

"Sure." She shrugged. *I'll only use it when I need to.* He smiled back at her. "This doesn't mean we're friends, this means we have a mutual agreement that even though we don't trust each other we can still be pleasant to one another." Adaline clarified.

"Oh, yeah...sure." He shifted. His ears drooped again.

"Well, what were you expecting? Just because it was wrong of me to say I hate you because of what happened when I was a kid doesn't mean we're friends now." Adaline retorted primly.

"W-well I mean, I wasn't *not* expecting that." He stumbled over his words. Glancing back up at Eric almost as if looking for help. "I just thought-"

Gilbert's horse slid in between them again. Adaline hadn't even noticed him slowing up.

"Eric seems moodier than usual. What's his issue?" Ryker fell silent and averted his eyes.

"I don't think Eric needs an issue to be moody." Adaline snickered. "He just is."

"Maybe he's tired, we didn't get a lot of sleep last night." Gilbert offered. He gently nudged Ryker, trying to get him to partake in the conversation too.

"We'll make camp in a few hours." Eric called back. "It'll probably be nearing sundown by then."

Adaline

Surprisingly, they made camp about the same time Eric said they would.

It was a quaint little grove, not too far off the road, with a stream running throughout the forest and branches covering overhead.

Ryker and Gilbert were already making themselves comfortable. They'd grabbed their packs and plopped down beside each other while Eric tied the horses to a tree.

Adaline sat down nearby and fidgeted with her skirt.

"Ryker, Adaline, get some sticks to start a fire. Gilbert, why don't you find something for dinner." Ryker didn't hesitate to open his pack and grab a few knives, which he shoved in his boots and underneath his sleeves, but Gilbert started complaining.

"Awh, must I? I'm sore from riding all day, can't we just eat the rations?"

"No. Those are for when we don't have time to hunt or scavenge." Eric grumbled. "This area is bountiful. You'll find the food tonight."

With a grin, Adaline followed Ryker, who was already heading out.

They weaved around trees for a while, picking up sticks, twigs and pretty much any kindling.

They'd made it pretty far away from camp before they'd decided to turn back around. Both of them had traveled pretty much in silence.

Ryker led the way, he'd been leaving markings in the trees, so they knew which way they came from, until he stopped and glanced around.

"Uhm..." He shifted the kindling in his arms.

"You didn't get us lost, did you?" Adaline would've put her hands on her hips if they weren't full.

"I refuse to answer. Uh.... The stream is this way, so we'll go this way and follow the stream." Adaline rolled her eyes and followed him.

Being lost in a forest wasn't on her bucket list. It was far more eerie than the night before.

She could hear branches creaking, seemingly louder than they should be. Their feet shuffling through detritus, squirrels chattering, leaves rustling, wind whistling around trunks. Everything seemed so much louder than it should've been.

She lost her footing on a root and tumbled straight into Ryker's back. They tumbled into a pile of leaves, dropping both of their gatherings on the ground.

Something swept them upward.

"*Ulp!*" Before Adaline knew what was going on, both she and Ryker were caught in a net, suspended fifteen feet in the air.

Chapter 22

Caught in an old hunter's trap was not how he'd seen his night ending, especially not with Adaline.

The worst part was, Ryker was stuck facing the ground, with Adaline stuck on top of him, her elbow dug into his back.

"Well, this is wonderful." She grumbled. "Absolutely brilliant, Ryker."

"I wasn't the one who tripped! This is your fault!" Ryker groaned. "And would you please move your elbow!"

"I wasn't the one who got us lost! And I can't move my elbow! You want to know why?" She shifted and it managed to elevate some of the pressure, but it was still uncomfortable. "Because we're stuck in a net with very little wiggle room!"

"Trust me, I know!" Ryker couldn't reach any of his knives, his hands were pinned underneath him. Besides, he'd only brough six, two in each sleeve and one in each boot.

"I hate you; you know that?" She hissed.

"The feeling's mutual." Ryker squirmed underneath.

"Okay, it doesn't matter whose fault this is, even though it's yours, what do we do now?" Adaline asked.

"I don't know." Ryker admitted. "Wait until Gilbert and Eric come looking for us, I guess."

Adaline huffed. "You really are amazing at problem-solving, aren't you?"

The two sat in silence for a while, listening to the forest around them.

Animals crunching around in the undergrowth. Wind whistling through the branches and playing with the leaves. The water in the stream sloshing not too far away.

"So, you can't reach your knives." Adaline broke the peacefulness of the night. "But perhaps I can."

"No." Ryker snapped, almost immediately after she said it. "There's no way, I'm letting you touch me enough to get one of my knives. That stupid ring could burn me."

"You really hate me that much?" Adaline asked.

"You hate me just the same!" He exclaimed. "Eric will find us."

"You really trust him that much?" Her voice softened.

"I haven't got anyone else, other than Gilbert of course." Ryker admitted. "I owe him a lot."

She didn't say anything after that. *Good. Let her stew on that for a while.* This time, it stayed silent, until something strange caught his ears. A shifting in the distance.

A horrifying thought entered his mind.

"Adaline, do you think this is a butcher's trap?" Ryker thought back to the night in the upper city. When the drunk mentioned they raised the price for elven ears. "They're gonna chop my ears off. They're going to sell them to collectors. My ears are going to be mounted on a wall." Ryker shifted.

"I thought part-elven ears were too short to be worth anything monumental."

"They upped the price. Besides, my ears are almost as long as a full-bloods, so unless they compare and contrast, no one is going to notice my ears are, in fact, *not* full-blood."

"Don't panic, Ryker. To be honest, it does look like a butcher's trap, but it could be a hunter." Ryker could tell she was trying to be reassuring, but it wasn't helping.

"Don't panic? I like my ears very much, thank you. I don't want them mounted on a wall somewhere." Ryker sighed. "Knowing my past, it'll be Helga's wall." *Right above the cane of punishment I'll bet.* Ryker thought miserably.

"It's going to be fine. You're the one who said you trusted Eric, now follow through with it." Adaline assured. Ryker rolled his eyes.

"You're not the one whose ears are gonna be mounted on a wall." He hissed.

He wished he were caught in the trap with Gilbert, Gilbert was his safety net. He was always reassuring, and he knew Gilbert would rather die than let a butcher get to Ryker.

The crunching in the distance started to come closer. Before Ryker could properly register what was coming, they were surrounded by bald men in orange and white robes. Acolytes of Surach.

"Or an acolyte trap." Adaline muttered above him. "Who feels stupid now?"

"You know what, Adaline? You're the one who should feel stupid."

"Why's that?" She asked mockingly. Ryker's cheeks heated and he gave up the attempt.

"Oh, just shut up."

The acolytes spoke in a language Ryker didn't understand. Before he knew it, they sent a fireball that seared the rope that attached the net to the tree.

The two fell free from the net, with Adaline landing on top of Ryker. Everything that didn't hurt before, hurt him now. After Adaline got off him, Ryker groaned and rolled onto his knees. He pulled two of his knives from his sleeves and looked up.

They were surrounded by ten acolytes, all of them were bald, wearing the same orange and white robes. None of them spoke, they just stared.

"Adaline?" Ryker stood up next to her. "What do we do?"

Before Adaline could respond the acolytes threw strange red dust in her eyes.

"Gah!" She dropped to her knees, rubbing her eyes. "It burns!" She shrieked.

Without thinking, Ryker threw his knife at the acolyte with the dust. His knife found a home in his chest. He fell to the ground, clutching at it.

Before Ryker could figure out his next move, something jabbed him in the neck. He slashed his knife at whatever poked him. He ended up stabbing a different acolyte in the arm.

He let out a howl. Ryker planted his foot into his stomach, sending him backwards, holding his bleeding arm.

None of the others made any moves, they all just stared at him, like they expected him to drop dead at any moment.

He stumbled back and put himself in front of Adaline who was still recovering from the dust in her eyes. Ryker's neck burned as his knuckles turned white around his knife's handle.

After a minute, he started to get dizzy, the acolytes started multiplying. He blinked and shook his head as spots started appearing in his vision. *What'd they stick me with?*

A wave of nausea hit him as he dropped to his knees and his knife fell from his grip. He was expecting to see Gilbert and Eric barge into the fray, but darkness came instead.

Chapter 23

Eric and Gilbert sat alone in the grove, they'd been waiting for hours for Ryker and Adaline to return, but they hadn't. They both sat facing each other, both knowing something was wrong, but neither wanting to admit it.

"We should go after them, neither of them have experience in the woodland." Gilbert spoke up. "I can't believe we let Ryker go off by himself, he doesn't know how the woodland works. There are poachers who would chop him up and sell him bit by bit."

"He isn't by himself. He has Adaline." Eric's brow furrowed. "And he can handle himself, you know that as well as I do."

"How much experience does Adaline have in the woodland? And they would probably know how to handle an elf. I've heard there are drugs that work specifically for elves." Gilbert pointed out.

Eric shook his head and stood up.

"You can forfeit the big brother act now, Gilbert. We'll go and find them." *Thank goodness.* Gilbert was relieved as he followed Eric where Ryker and Adaline had left.

Eric muttered an incantation into his cane, it lit up, illuminating the surrounding area. He muttered something else, but Gilbert didn't know what it meant, but he didn't see any changes anywhere.

They hadn't gotten very far when they noticed markings on some trees.

"See? Ryker knew what he was doing." Eric said as he traced along the bark. Gilbert huffed. He knew Ryker could fend for himself, but that didn't stop him from worrying.

He glanced down at the ground. There were footprints going forward, but none coming back.

"Hm, do you think they just got lost?" Gibert asked following the line of trees that had markings in them.

"Maybe." Eric took the lead, scanning the ground with his light.

They traveled in silence for a while, Gilbert scratched some new markings into the trees so they wouldn't get lost, but there seemed to be a plethora of large gaps between Ryker's marks, so it was no wonder they got lost.

All Gilbert could hear was the snapping of twigs beneath their feet and the eerie whistling of the wind through the trees.

Out of nowhere Eric turned sideways and started following a different trail, leaving Gilbert in the dark alone. *I really need a drink.*

"Eric! The markings go this way." He called after him. Eric didn't slow, he didn't even turn around. *Perhaps he sees something I can't.*

Gilbert knew little about creation magic, but perhaps there was more to it than just being handy in a jam.

Gilbert waited until the light from his staff fled from view, he'd expected Eric to come back and get him, but he didn't.

Not wanting to be left alone in the creepy woods, he followed after Eric. Trying to navigate in the dark was much more difficult than he expected. He walked into spiderwebs and stumbled over roots.

"Eric!" He called.

"Over here!" He heard his voice cry out. *Thank goodness.*

Gilbert headed toward his voice until he saw the light from his staff creep around the trunk of a tree.

Eric had set his cane down beside him and he was knelt on the ground with something in his hand. The light from the cane also revealed a dead bald man in orange and white robes. He had a knife sticking out of his chest.

Gilbert knelt down and inspected the knife, it was one of Rykers, he was certain. The thin but sturdy blade had gone all the way in, leaving only the golden handle exposed. *Gross.*

"They must have been ambushed." He started to pull the knife free. *Ryker will want this back.*

"No, I think it was a trap." Eric said, grabbing his cane and standing up. Gilbert took Ryker's knife out of the acolyte and shouldered up next to him. There was a net with burnt ends on the ground that was partially covered by leaves.

"And there was this." Eric held up another one of Ryker's knives and his dragon necklace, as well as his earrings, and another pair of silver earrings and a silvery ring with a ruby gem. Gilbert assumed those were Adaline's.

He handed Ryker's things to Gilbert. "I believe it's safe to assume the acolytes of Surach have them."

Gilbert didn't like the sound of that, but it was also hard to believe. Unless they got the drop on him, Ryker could've handled twenty of them easily.

"So, how do we find them?" Gilbert asked. Eric's lips quirked.

"The same way we found this. We track."

Chapter 24

Ryker awoke, wherever he was lying was beyond uncomfortable. Head pounding, he forced his eyes open.

He was locked in a cage that seemed to be made for a large dog. It was small enough that he wouldn't have been able to sit up or stretch out, not that he wanted to, and his wrists and his ankles were secured by metal shackles. *Wonderful.*

He struggled to take in what was on the outside of his kennel.

It was a stone room that was dimly lit by only two torches. He could make out some moss growing on the walls. He could see the outline of other cages across from his, varying in size, but they looked empty.

There was a shuffle beside him. He turned his gaze toward it.

Someone sat in a cage similar to Ryker's, but it was big enough for them to sit up. Whoever it was was bound the same way Ryker was, metal shackles on their wrists and ankles.

"Ryker?" They whispered. It was a female voice.

"Adaline?" He whispered back. Squinting, he was able to see her outline, but the shadows from the other cages on the other side of Ryker's blocked a lot of the dim torchlight.

"It's me. I'm glad you're awake, honestly you were starting to scare me." Adaline shifted to the end of her cage. "My eyes still burn, but I can see again. How are you?"

Ryker felt awful. His throat was dry, there were spots in his eyes, and he could hardly move his limbs.

"Groggy. Where are we?"

"I have no idea, they knocked me out before they moved us, but I think it's safe to assume we're in a temple of some sort, seeing as they're acolytes."

"Marvelous." Ryker muttered. He shivered and coughed.

"Well, that doesn't sound good." Adaline retorted.

"It's just a side-effect from whatever they stuck me with." He assured her. "I'll be fine." He took a few breaths in from his nose. He needed to collect his thoughts and push anything else out of his mind.

There was a scraping sound and more light peered in from the right. Ryker glanced over. The stone wall had opened, revealing two stone doors, and three acolytes trudged in, one of which had a metal poker in hand. They were all bald, wearing the same robes, and equally ugly.

Ryker rolled from his side to his back to get a better view of them.

"So, he's the one who killed Corbyn?" One of them asked.

"And injured Armin. However, the drug worked faster on him than the others." Another one answered.

"So, he's fast, but his constitution is weak. He's too thin. Will he really be a worthy sacrifice?" The one with the poker questioned.

"Well, the woman is well enough, perhaps we should rid ourselves of him." The first one replied. *I do not like the sound of that.* Ryker thought miserably. He glanced at Adaline. She sat still, listening to the conversation.

"Stick him. I want to see what the new drug does." The first one ordered the one with the poker. "He's too feisty. Can't risk him getting away."

"And ensure the shackles on the witch are secure, we don't want her getting free either." The other one chimed in.

The one with the poker in hand edged closer to his cage. He stabbed through the bars. Ryker wanted to dodge, but he hardly moved. The poker stabbed him right in the neck.

It didn't take long before Ryker's head started swimming and black dots appeared in his vision. He squeezed his eyes shut, wishing the nausea would go away.

"Did you stick him?" One of them asked.

"Sure did." The one above him sniggered.

"I wonder what side-effects the new drug has."

Ryker didn't hear anything else after that. His prison world disappeared into darkness.

Chapter 25

Eric

Eric and Gilbert were tracking the acolytes' footprints with the light from Eric's cane. It was a large trail.

Eric had been able to deduce that there were probably about ten acolytes that had taken them. His concern for his crew started to overwhelm his thoughts.

If there were too many acolytes there was no way they would be able to free them.

It probably wasn't too smart of him to send Adaline and Ryker together, not after he'd heard about the ring incident. Ryker had brought it up in hopes for Eric to convince her to take it off. He'd tried to tell him that Adaline was stubborn, and Ryker should try to befriend her, but from how forlorn and quiet Ryker was before they made camp Eric guessed that didn't go well.

They followed the main footprints and the obvious trail until a different trail broke off. A set of footprints and what appeared to be an indentation of someone being dragged away. *Odd.* He thought. That trail was fresh.

Eric started following that trail, Gilbert followed quietly. It was also odd that he didn't ask any questions, usually he would. Eric wasn't complaining.

The footprints began to appear more and more fresh.

Gilbert halted to a stop.

"Hear that?" he said in a faint whisper.

Eric, knowing the footprints were fresh, dimmed the light and readied his cane. He braced himself behind a tree, peering out he saw

Ryker unconscious tied to a tree. An acolyte stood above him with a knife in hand.

He motioned for Gilbert to follow his lead. Gilbert immediately took cover behind a tree and drew one of his crossbows.

Right after Gilbert got into position, Eric ran out and clubbed the acolyte in the head. He dropped the knife to the ground.

Eric grabbed him by the back of his neck and tore him away, swiping his legs out from underneath him. Eric pinned the acolyte underneath him with a knee in his back and started pushing his head into the ground. He felt angrier the more the acolyte struggled.

"Where is Adaline?" he demanded.

Gilbert ran to Ryker and started untying him. Passing Eric an uncertain glance and an almost pitying look to the acolyte.

Ryker's eyes cracked open, and he coughed a few times. Gilbert tossed the rope aside and scooted next to Ryker, whose head plopped onto his shoulder.

"Ryker," Gilbert softened his voice when he spoke. "Where is Adaline?"

"She's somewhere." Ryker replied sleepily. "In a cage." His eyes closed again.

"Yeah, he's completely out of it." Gilbert brushed the strands that were loose from Ryker's braid out his face.

"That's fine." Eric assured; his voice was almost a growl. He applied more pressure to the acolyte's neck. "We'll just get answers from him."

"Hold on, Eric. The acolyte would probably rather die than betray the others. I don't think you're going to make him talk." Gilbert sighed.

Eric hated to admit it, but he was right. Acolytes were a loyal bunch.

"We'll just follow the trail and hope it isn't a decoy." He alleviated some of the pressure off the acolyte's neck.

"What about Ryker? We can't leave him by himself. Not when he's like this." Eric's jaw clenched. He hadn't thought of that.

The half-elf's complexion was ashen, his breathing was labored, and there were two strange marks on his neck, but other than that he seemed fine.

"He just needs to sleep off whatever they stuck him with. He'll be fine." The acolyte snickered beneath him. Eric shoved his face further into the dirt as rage pulsed through his veins.

"Eric!" Gilbert intervened. "He's just trying to waste our time. We need a plan." He moved Ryker off his shoulder and set him on the ground. Eric took a deep breath.

Gilbert was right. His emotions were blinding his judgment. *So much for keeping them away from this job.* He thought bitterly.

"Okay. You take Ryker back to camp. Stay with him until he's awake." Eric glanced back toward the first trail they were following before. "I'll follow the trail and see where it leads. Do you think you'll be able to find me again?"

"I'm sure Ryker can. He's always been better at tracking than me." Gilbert nodded. "What about the acolyte?"

"First off, Ryker can't come with you. Someone needs to look after the horses, we've left them alone for a while, and I doubt he'll be mobile any time soon. Just wait until he's up." Gilbert looked a little unsure at first, but he took one look at Ryker and nodded in agreement. "I have an idea for the acolyte." Eric grabbed his cane and clubbed him in the back of the head, knocking him out.

Gilbert, obviously knowing where it was going, went and grabbed the rope. Together, Eric and Gilbert tied him to the tree Ryker was tied to.

After that, Gilbert picked Ryker up off the ground. Eric cast a quick spell to make their dragon pendants light the way for them.

"Don't do anything I wouldn't do." Gilbert warned before starting back for camp with Ryker slung over his shoulder. Eric rubbed the polished handle of his cane. *I suppose it's down to me.*

Chapter 26

Adaline was still sitting in her cage. The itching in her eyes

had subsided and her vision was cleared.

She was starting to regret not trusting Ryker sooner. She supposed his comment about Eric and Gilbert being all he had helped her see a softer side of him.

He had been nice to her, for the little time they spoke. She was cynical, that she knew, but Ryker hadn't done anything to deserve her crass attitude. Although, being half-elf, it seemed he was accustomed to that.

She huddled in the corner of her cage and stared out at the door. She wanted the acolytes to bring Ryker back. She felt alone.

Ryker was the only other form of life that was in the room before, so even though he was knocked out for most of it, his sputters, coughs, and slight movements brought comfort. She'd had hope that when Ryker woke up, they could figure out a way to escape, but then the acolytes had shown up.

They'd taken him somewhere almost immediately after they jabbed him. She didn't know where he'd been taken, or what was being done to him. She wasn't even fully sure why they'd taken him. *He didn't have a good enough constitution? What is that supposed to mean? He seemed fine, other than whatever they stuck him with.*

Adaline had been pondering what that meant by that for hours now. She knew she needed to think of a way out, but something in her kept drifting back to that. An instinct of sorts.

She couldn't reach her magic, not with the shackles. Whether they knew that, or it was just an unlucky coincidence, she couldn't tell. *Either I have the worst luck, or the acolytes are smarter than they look.*

While Adaline pondered, her stomach growled.

The answer hit her in the face like the clapper striking a bell. *The sacrifices need a good constitution. If I'm without food, it weakens my physical health.*

No food would fit through the bars of her cage, which would mean they would have to unlock the cage to give her some. Giving her an opportunity to escape. *Then I would just need to find Ryker and we could just run, assuming the acolytes are as dumb as I believe.*

Now Adaline had a plan, she just needed an acolyte to put it into motion.

As luck would have it, probably about an hour later, the stone doors scraped open, and an acolyte entered. He had no tray of food, though. The door scraped shut again once he made it to her cage.

Adaline's stomach growled as if on cue. The acolyte eyed her.

"Excuse me, could I please get something to eat."

"No." He growled. His voice had the rasp of two stones being scraped together.

"Without food, I'll be too weak to make a worthy sacrifice, don't you think?" His jaw ticked and he stood there for a moment. With a scoff, he spun on his heel and headed back towards the door.

It started to scrape open again when the acolyte made it about halfway to it. *That was easy. Perhaps too easy.* She thought.

After he left, she was all by herself again. She was hoping that her plan was working, and the acolyte would unlock her cage. She was relying on instinct to get her through the rest.

Her instincts hadn't let her down yet, then again, Pastow wasn't as rough as she'd heard Hadune was.

When she originally agreed to join the job, she was expecting Eric to protect her. After all, she was only a healer.

Sure, she could drop someone into a coma, only for a few minutes at most. She couldn't even reach her magic, not with the shackles, and other than her magic, her instincts had pretty much protected her her whole life.

A few minutes later the acolyte returned. He had a tray of food with him. It didn't look appetizing.

When he made it about halfway to her cage, the doors scraped closed again.

The acolyte kicked her cage.

"Get back." He ordered. Adaline pressed her back up against the bars of her cage. Though it probably looked as if she didn't move at all.

He knelt and produced a key. Her heart pounded in her throat. *This is it.* He swung the door of the cage open.

She launched her foot into the tray of slop, smashing it into his face.

Adaline crawled swiftly out of her cage.

The acolyte was trying to sling the gunk from his eyes. He rolled onto his stomach and tried to crawl away from her.

While he was blinded, Adaline got on top of him and wrapped the chain of her shackles around his neck. She wished she could feel his heart race, but she couldn't.

He got up on his knees and struggled against her, flinging her around. She held them tight around his neck until he stopped moving and went limp underneath her.

She shoved his unconscious body to the side. Adaline sighed. *Now what?*

She tiptoed over to about the halfway mark, that she'd seen the door open for the acolyte before. There was a creaking sound, but the door didn't open. *How am I supposed to get out of this?*

Just as she thought that a blue-gold light swirled behind her. She spun around. A glowing blue portal with golden particles swirling through it. After a minute, someone fell through, and the portal faded. Eric popped his head up from the floor.

"Yes!" He exclaimed, pumping his fist in the air like a child.

"Eric?!" Adaline said incredulously. He popped up from the floor to his feet.

"I've been working on a teleportation spell, and it finally worked." He dusted himself off and picked his cane off the floor. "Where are we?" He asked.

"You don't know? How did you teleport here if you don't know?" Adaline asked. He dug in his pocket and held out his hand, revealing two silver stud earrings. She didn't even know her earrings had come off.

"I still can't believe that worked!" He grinned. Adaline couldn't hold back her giggle. Then she remembered something.

"Ryker! I don't know where he is. They took him out of his cell a while ago." Eric just scratched his chin.

"What if I told you we are way ahead of you on that?" He smirked.

"Where? Is he okay?" She asked. Eric raised his neat brows.

"Seems someone has taken a liking to him. I knew you two would get along in time." Adaline rolled her eyes. Saying she liked him would be generous. She could see herself getting through the job with him without any further disagreements, but she couldn't see herself actually *liking* him. He's an elf, after all.

"Now," Eric said. "Let's get out of here." Her brow furrowed as she looked around the dark room.

"How?" His smirk fell sideways, making a befuddled face at her. His brown eyes squinted in the darkness.

"That's a good question."

Chapter 27

Eric

Eric and Adaline were still in the dungeon of the temple.

She'd explained what happened while Eric inspected the door. He wished he could simply teleport back to Gilbert and Ryker, but he didn't have any items that belonged to them, and he was too far away to even link their necklaces.

He ran his hands over the rough surface of the door. He could feel magic pulsing from the other side. It felt like elemental magic. *Perhaps he sealed it from the outside before he blacked out.*

Adaline was still poking around where she'd sworn the door had opened for him before.

Eric had an idea. If he was right, the door was being held shut by vines. *If I could create something sharp enough to cut through them, we could get out.* He moved his cane out in front of him. *Then I suppose we must do my least favorite thing, wing it.* He wished Gilbert and Ryker were here. He preferred plans, they preferred going with the flow.

He imagined the other side of the door. He didn't know exactly what it looked like, but he was certain he could imagine it close enough.

Stone with moss, most likely more torches. Maybe some stairs headed up towards the main room.

He closed his eyes and imagined a golden saw forming in front of the vines. He moved it closer until he could hear the saw cutting across the vines.

Snap!

The vines gave way. The door scraped against the floor, opening towards Eric. He jumped out of the way before it hit him. He allowed the saw to dissolve into golden dust that now decorated the floor in front of the door.

"What did you do?" Adaline whispered, creeping up beside him.

"Doesn't matter. Let's just get out of here." Eric readied his cane and crept out of the dungeon.

He'd imagined it surprisingly accurately. Better lighting, the same stony walls, with moss growing in places and vines seeping between cracks in the walls. There was a staircase, but it wasn't exactly how he'd seen it. In his head he'd imagined a spiral staircase behind a wooden door, here there was just a large column of stairs that took up the whole wall. There was a wooden door at the top of them, though.

Adaline and Eric snuck silently through the large corridor. When they made it to the center of the room the door scraped shut again.

"May I just say, one, that is extremely noisy, two, that is an awful door for a dungeon. Imagine when you're trying to leave and accidentally step on the middle of the floor more than once and let all the prisoners out. I mean, it's completely unethical. Who thought of this?" Eric murmured to Adaline.

"Well, did you see all the cages in there? I don't think fleeing through the door is an option." She paused for a moment. "You know, that does raise a good question. How did they not accidentally open the door when walking back and forth?" Adaline knelt and inspected the floor. "It isn't like there's a certain tile that we stepped on.

"Why does that matter?" Eric asked. He eyed the door and just as he had suspected, there were vines that had been sawed in half growing from the cracks beside the strange door frame.

"Well, it doesn't. I was just curious." She stood back up. "You were the one who brought up the door in the first place." He ignored her and drew his cane out in front of him. He imagined his own golden vines connecting to the real ones. They crossed over to one another and seeped underneath the door, sealing it from both sides, rather than just the outside.

"Smart." Adaline said, only half paying attention to what he was doing. She seemed more interested in trying to figure out how they got in and out without accidentally opening the door constantly.

"I mean, if they just stood there instead of walking straight out, would it continuously open and shut?" Adaline walked in circles on the other side of the room, staring at the floor.

"I think we're just thinking about this too much and it's simple. Can we go now?" Eric skipped over the center of the floor, afraid of accidentally triggering the door and possibly snapping his golden vines. His creation magic vines probably were not as sturdy as the vines the acolyte used.

He hooked Adaline by the arm and dragged her up the stairs. The wooden door had rusty metal hinges and rusting metal bindings that held the planks together. Eric tried to look through the slots between the wooden boards, but they were too thin.

"What do we do now?" Adaline whispered, trying to see through the door. "I'm still shackled, I can't feel if anyone is out there with these."

"Oh, I didn't think about that. Let me see." She held out her hands. Eric found the keyhole along the wrist bindings and felt around, trying to get a feel for its interior. Once he was pretty sure he could replicate the key, he leaned his cane on the stone wall.

He drew in a deep breath and held out his hands. Golden dust seemed to appear out of thin air and floated between his hands. He focused his magic and morphed the dust into a key shape. He added more layers to make it look older and thicker, then removed some to make it smaller with a few notches. He supposed he was just showing off at this point. He hadn't used creation magic like that for a long time.

He messed with it until it felt like it matched the keyhole. He allowed the key to drop into his hand. It had a slight glow to it, but other than that it just looked like a golden key.

The shackles made a clicking sound as he turned the key and the cuff slid off her wrist. He did the same with her other wrist. She caught them by the chain before they clinked onto the floor. She set them down behind her. They made a soft clunking sound when they hit the floor, but it wasn't anything anyone on the other side of the door would hear.

She put one hand against the wall and closed her eyes. After a few moments she opened her eyes and took her hand off the wall.

"They're not in there, but there are a bunch above us." She whispered. Eric opened the door. He could feel his magic calling him back to the surface.

Creation mages drew their power from sunlight. At night his magic was weaker, that was the reason he relied so much on his cane. His grandfather told him it had a sunfire stone molded inside of it. He tried to ask him how, as sunfire stones were so bright, but his grandfather never told him.

If his magic was calling him above ground, that must mean the sun is up. He hoped Gilbert had gotten Ryker back to camp and was on his way.

The room on the other side of the door was a lot like what Eric had originally imagined. Stony walls, moss, and a spiral staircase in a door frame. He could hear indistinct talking up above them. He looked back at Adaline.

"How many?" He mouthed. She held up five fingers. *Great.* He muttered. He could feel his power picking up with every move closer towards the outdoors. *I bet if we can take care of those five, I'll be able to link the necklaces and teleport.* Eric was being optimistic, perhaps too much so. He was slightly fatigued. None of them had gotten much sleep, and using magic was draining. Even with sunlight nearby it wasn't likely he would be able to teleport, but he bet he could still link their necklaces.

Eric started to creep toward the stairs when Adaline caught him by the arm.

"I can drop two, if you could figure something out for the other three." Eric slipped halfway up the steps until he could see the open door. He could see two of the acolytes. They clearly didn't seem to notice their friend that was missing. He readied his cane and motioned for Adaline to drop them. After a few agonizing minutes of Eric holding his breath, one acolyte dropped. A few seconds later, the one beside him dropped.

Eric busted through the door, a blast of energy already forming in one of the eyes of his cane. He blasted it at the nearest acolyte. None of them were ready for it, so the bald man dropped to the ground with a smoking chest.

The acolyte closest to Eric created a fireball in his hand. Before he could throw it, Eric smashed his cane into his face. The dragon's snout left a mark on his forehead, and he collapsed next, the fireball dissolving in his hand.

Something flew into Eric's side, knocking him off his feet. He hit the wall and slid to the ground. He didn't want to get back up, but he knew he had to.

With a grunt, he crawled up to his knees and faced the last acolyte. He had a fireball in one hand, and Eric's cane in the other. Eric hadn't even realized he dropped it.

He gave a single sigh, he felt closer to the sunlight than he was before. He could see a slight golden glow gleaming through the diamonds of his cane.

The acolyte let the fireball dissolve in his hand and lifted Eric's cane over his head.

"You've done enough damage, wretch."

Chapter 28

The acolyte prepared to bash Eric's head with his own cane.

Eric's eyes flashed gold. He popped off the ground and grabbed the cane and fed power into it. The acolyte's eyes widened as the cane sent fiery power straight through him.

The acolyte's eyes flashed their own shade of gold. His joints locked up and smoke rolled out of his nostrils.

By the time his body hit the floor he was nothing but a pile of charred bones.

The three acolytes that were unconscious showed no signs of stirring.

"Adaline?" He called back down the steps. It didn't take long for her to pop her head into the door frame.

"I'm kind of surprised you're still alive." She looked around the room. It matched the rest of the temple well.

The same mossy walls and cracked floors. There was a cooking pot hanging over a fire in the corner. It was surrounded by chairs. There were shelves filled with strange artifacts and odd things in jars. Torches lined the walls, lighting the room much better than the others. There was one other wooden door that most likely led to a much bigger cavern, if Eric was lucky enough to guess the temple's layout that is. It was probably one of the cozier rooms in the disturbing temple.

Adaline glanced at the pile of ash and bones in front of Eric.

"Seems an old dog can learn new tricks." Eric fought back a smile. He felt much closer to the sun now. He wondered if he was back on ground level or just closer to it.

"We should barricade the door." He said, brushing off her comment. She did another inspection of the room.

"With what, exactly?" Eric motioned toward the chairs that surrounded the pot. She gave him an annoyed look.

"Make the best out of what we have. I need to figure something else out while you figure that out." This time Eric didn't hide his smirk. Her irritation amused him.

Begrudgingly, she started to move the chairs to block the door.

Eric knew that it was no use. They were elemental mages and there was probably no way a few chairs would do anything to keep them out, but he needed Adaline preoccupied so he could focus.

He stepped over the ashes and sat down in the middle of the room. Crossing his legs and laying his cane in his lap. He looked into the dragon's eyes.

He focused his energy on finding the matching necklaces and connecting to them. If he managed to do it right, they would be able to communicate through their thoughts. He'd done it a few times before, but never from this distance. It was draining, too, so he only ever did it if he felt he had no other options.

After a few minutes there was a spark. That flickered in the eye of his dragon head cane. Suddenly, he felt a familiar connection, one he hadn't felt in a long time.

Gilbert? Ryker? Eric thought. He felt a wave of shock and confusion. Then another wave of strange, contented, happiness.

Eric? Gilbert's thoughts reverberated in his head. He forgot how hard it was to get used to. *How are you- oh! I remember now. Are you okay? Did you find Adaline?* Eric was slightly relieved to hear Gilbert's voice. At least that meant he and Ryker were both okay.

Woah, I completely forgot this was a thing. Ryker's voice danced in Eric's head. His thoughts sounded strangely at ease. *This is so cool. Why don't we do this more often?*

Ignore him. Gilbert piped up. *Are you and Adaline, okay?*

We're fine. We are trapped in a temple currently. How are you guys?

"What are you doing?" Adaline asked. He glanced up at her. She had her hands on her hips and her icy stare seemed to glare through him.

"Talking to Ryker and Gilbert. One second." He turned his attention back to the conversation in his head. She scoffed and rolled her eyes.

"Creation mages." He heard her mutter.

Ryker, are you still with the horses? Eric asked.

Uh, Yah. I have a question though. He sounded completely unfazed by anything that was going on. *Do horses really make glue? If so, how?*

He felt a twinge of annoyance from Gilbert, but it was quickly overtaken by concern.

Well technically the horses don't actually make glue. Eric replied, amusing Ryker just to get to Gilbert. *Their hooves are usually-*

Okay. Ryker cut his thoughts off. *Why is it called glue though?*

Ryker, can we talk about this later? Gilbert's thoughts echoed in his head again.

The glue? Sure. Speaking of why things are called what they are, why is cheese called cheese? Ryker's thoughts were still too casual for what was going on. *Cheese sounds amazing right now. I'm really hungry. Can we get cheese when you guys get back?* Eric's head started to throb. Another rough side effect of magic overuse.

Gilbert. Where are you? Eric tried to shift the focus back to the problem at hand.

I'm right by the acolyte Ryker killed, but the trail is gone. He could feel Gilbert's distress in his head.

Okay. Stay near the acolyte. I'll have to teleport somehow

Teleport? Both Gilbert and Ryker thought at the same time. Gilbert's thoughts were coming through much clearer than Ryker's. With the way he was acting, it seemed Ryker wasn't all there.

That's new. When did you learn that? Gilbert asked.

Ryker's thoughts emerged before Eric could answer. *Yeah, that's cool and all, but I was talking about cheese. I'm pretty sure cheese has nothing to do with teleportation.*

Why are you so fixated on cheese? Gilbert asked, immediately getting distracted.

Cheese is delicious. It's supposed to go great with... like... wine and crackers, I think. I've actually never had wine before. Isn't that like a drink for the rich snobs? Crackers are good, though, but I've never had cheese with them.

Ryker! Move away from the cheese. Eric reprimanded. *I will get you all the cheese and crackers you want, if you could just, please focus for two minutes.* Eric's headache worsened by the minute. He didn't have a lot of time, and if he was going to have to teleport, he'd need to cut off the connection as soon as possible.

What about the wine? Can I try some wine too?

Why would you want— I guess you can. Both of you stay where you are, that's an order. Ryker... Gee, I don't know, drink some water. Get it together.

Hold on— Gilbert's voice left his head as Eric cut off the connection. He stood up. It seemed like the connection had gotten him nowhere. At least he knew he would have to teleport.

He looked back at Adaline. She was pulling some twigs out of her boot.

"Wait! Where did you get those?" He rushed over and took them from her hands.

"My boot?" She answered, puzzled. He inspected one of the sticks. They looked like they were from the same trees that filled the forest. "They might be from some of the kindling Ryker, and I had." She continued, but she still looked confused. Her eyes lit up. "Can you teleport to the tree it belongs to?"

That's exactly what Eric was thinking.

"Only one way to find out."

Chapter 29

Adaline stood watch by the door while Eric sat cross legged on the floor with his cane in his lap, trying to summon a portal. Neither of them were sure if it would work, but they didn't have any other option.

If the portal didn't work, they would be stuck with no way out. Eric had said since he was closer to the sun, he might be able to make one, despite his headache. After a few minutes a sharp crackle caught her ear. She spun around.

A small portal had appeared in front of Eric. It wasn't big enough for either of them to fit through, but she could tell by the sweat that beaded his forehead that he was working on that.

Unfortunately, he wouldn't have much time.

She heard the scuffle of steps coming down the corridor behind the door. It sounded like the acolytes were ready for the sacrifice.

She gathered her magic and listened to their heartbeats. Twelve acolytes were headed towards the door.

"Eric!" She whispered harshly. "We have company!" She saw a flash of panic when he opened his eyes. He looked at the portal. It had grown, but not big enough. He squeezed his eyes shut again. The portal started to flicker. It grew a bit more, but it was only about the size of a large dog door.

The doorknob wiggled, but it was jammed by the chair she had moved in front of it. *Crap!* She looked back at Eric and his portal. He looked exhausted from where he sat. It seemed the portal wasn't going to get any bigger.

"Rueben!" A voice outside the door called. "Let us in!" One of the acolytes groaned from the floor. She assumed that it was Rueben.

"Eric!" She whispered again. The portal hadn't really grown.

"What was that?" A different voice yelled from outside the door. Eric shot up from the floor and grabbed Adaline's wrist. A fireball flashed between the planks and hit the wooden door. The door burst into flames.

Before the acolytes could see them through the smoke and ash now drifting in the air, Eric shoved Adaline through the portal. It was a miracle she fit. Suddenly, she was sprawled out on some grass.

She sat up. Eric fell through the small portal next. He lay on his back in the grass, chest heaving.

They were back in the forest, but a part she didn't remember. Perhaps it just looked different in the daytime.

Sunlight now fell between the branches of the trees overhead, decorating the grass and giving it a faint glow.

"I can't believe we did that." Adaline was astounded. Eric scooted until he was seated in one of the patches of sun. He let out a sigh of relief.

"I suppose portal magic isn't exactly as complicated as I thought." He said, a little out of breath. She stood up and looked around.

"What do we do now?" Eric eyed her when she said that. He obviously wasn't in the mood to discuss planning.

"I'm going to rest for a while. Then I guess we should find the others." Eric paused for a moment. "Part of me just wants to sit here and let them find us, but I'm kind of worried. I don't know what they stuck him with, but all Ryker was talking about was cheese. Do you think he's okay?"

"Cheese?"

"And he said something about glue." Eric shrugged. "He was probably just hungry. Ryker is always hungry." He closed his eyes and leaned against a tree. "We'll figure it out when we do, I suppose."

Adaline

After about an hour Eric had used his magic to track down Gilbert. From there, they'd found the acolyte Eric had tied to a tree and taken him back to camp, where they found Ryker. He was still out of sorts. He'd eaten some crackers, when Gilbert had reminded him where they were, before Eric told him to try to sleep off what they stuck him with. After that Eric went to sleep while Gilbert stood guard over the acolyte.

Now the sun was starting to dip behind the far-off mountains. Adaline stood near the horses, Gilbert was still watching over the acolyte, who was tied to a tree and gagged. Ryker, who had woken not too long ago and seemed much better, stood off to the side. His back was to the small fire they had made.

She hated to admit it, but she owed him an apology. He couldn't help who he was, and she had no reason to punish him for something that was out of his control.

She swallowed her pride and walked over. He didn't turn as she approached, though it was evident he knew she was there.

"So." She eased over and leaned on the tree across from him. "I suppose I owe you a..." Her voice trailed off. Perhaps it was how her father raised her, but apologizing to an elf felt wrong, somehow.

"An apology?" He finished her sentence for her. She nodded. He looked at her expectantly.

"What?" He gave her an exasperated look.

"That's it?" He demanded. "I have to apologize *for* you?"

"What? The intention was there, was that not enough?" Now she was just messing with him. She understood Eric now, they both were funny when they were annoyed.

"No, that wasn't enough! You couldn't even say it!" He exclaimed. She put her hands up.

"Okay, okay." She chuckled. "I apologize for how mean I've been. You've proved I can trust you enough for this job." He let out an amused scoff.

"I see you lost the ring." He eyed her hand.

"Yeah, it came off after the acolytes knocked me out. I don't know where it went." She rubbed her finger where it usually was.

"So, colleagues for now?" He extended his hand.

"Colleagues for now." She clasped it. *Though I suppose you are slightly under me, being Eric's property and all.* She refrained from saying that out loud, but it was true. They were interrupted by Eric, who strolled over and pushed their hands apart in his usual grouchy demeanor.

"I'm glad you two are getting along, but the both of you have cost us valuable time, which on this mission isn't exactly expendable." He looked directly at Ryker when he said, "You of all people should be a bit more careful with how you choose to spend it, all things considered." Ryker averted his eyes.

"Well, we didn't *choose* to get captured." Adaline clarified. Eric rolled his eyes.

"Doesn't matter. I'm surprised you couldn't handle the acolytes." Eric looked Ryker up and down. "Perhaps you should lay off the crackers." Ryker couldn't contain his snicker that time. She saw a slight smile appear on Eric's face before he quickly covered it up with his perpetual frown.

"Since the both of you have cost us this much time, we will be traveling throughout the night, and we will not be stopping until we make it to Erith."

Chapter 30

In reality, Erith was a smaller city, but to the people from Pastow it was huge. It was a bit smaller than Hadune, but the difference wasn't really in size, it was in quality. The people in Erith were so much friendlier, you were a lot less likely to lose your wallet there, but that wasn't to say there weren't gangs that would most likely be interested in the dragon egg. He would need to keep a close eye on his crew.

He glanced behind him. Gilbert and Adaline rode their horses chatting back and forth, Ryker walked close behind. They'd tied the acolyte to his horse and Eric had sent a magic guide to take it back to Pastow. They left a note explaining where their acolyte problem was stemming from. Ryker had been walking ever since.

Unfortunately for him, Eric held true to his word. They only stopped to rest the horses. Eric did have to admit he was sore from riding so much, but Erith was coming up on the horizon.

Its large walls worked well to keep out any unwanted visitors, but the river that ran underneath the city was a security issue.

The city was built around a small mountain with a waterfall flowing into a river which flowed into a lake. It was split up much like Hadune with the lower class being housed down at the base of the mountain and the higher class working its way up towards the top.

Eric had been there multiple times when his father had taken him on business trips, and he knew how the city functioned. There were two entrances, one that led to the main market area, and one that led to the street where the inns were. There were usually guards that kept watch over both entrances.

Eric pulled to a stop when they came across the fork in the road that led them to the separate entrances. Adaline and Gilbert stopped their horses beside him. Ryker was still lagging behind.

"So, this is Erith?" Adaline spoke first. "It's much more magnificent than I thought it would be."

"Yeah. It's much cleaner than Hadune. That's for sure." Gilbert agreed.

Ryker appeared on the other side of Eric.

"Welcome to Erith." Eric announced. Ryker squinted up at the conurbation.

"It just looks like a lot of walking." He groaned miserably. Gilbert and Adaline chuckled at him.

"Not enjoying yourself, Ryker?" Eric questioned. Ryker glared up at him. He looked like he wanted to say something, but he just shook his head and turned his attention back to the city.

"Okay. Gilbert, Ryker, you two are going to go to the right entrance. Find a room at the Ivory cavern inn, we'll find you from there." Eric ordered. "Adaline and I are going left. We're going to get supplies and we'll meet you at the room." Gilbert shot Ryker with a mischievous grin. He dug his heel into his horse's side and took off at a gallop.

"Oh, Gilbert, wait up!" Ryker called as he raced after him. Adaline laughed as the two raced up the hill and disappeared behind the trees of the forest.

"Part of me feels bad for Ryker, but it's funny seeing those two argue." Adaline laughed again.

Eric nodded. "Now you know how I feel every day." He shifted in his saddle. "Let's go get these supplies so I can sleep."

Eric

Eric and Adaline strolled into the Ivory cavern's room.

It was a quant place, built entirely from dark colored wood. It was decorated with comfortable furniture.

Sofas surrounded a fireplace, creating an inviting seating area, three beds lined the wall across from them, and there was a wooden door in between the two of them, most likely a washroom.

Gilbert was sitting with his feet propped on the table, in the middle of the room and Ryker was sitting cross-legged on the floor. Adaline walked over and set her basket of supplies on the table. Eric followed suit and set his next to hers.

"Well, you two are awfully quiet." Adaline spoke up. Gilbert glanced at Ryker, who looked to be holding back laughter, like a child with a secret. Ryker looked far more energized than before.

"Ryker." Eric folded his arms over his chest.

"Mhm?" He replied sheepishly, not taking his eyes off the floor.

"You do realize you can't lie, don't you?" Eric remarked. "You two are hiding something. Out with it."

"Woah, hang on. How do you know we're hiding something?" Gilbert piped up. Eric rolled his eyes.

If there was one thing Ryker was bad at, it was hiding things. He could keep secrets for others, but when it came to hiding something for himself, he always gave himself up.

Something yipped from the wardrobe.

"What was that?" Adaline asked. Eric didn't wait for an answer. He made his way over to the wardrobe, where Ryker slid in front of him.

"It was nothing." Ryker said, pressing his back to the closet. Something scratched at the door behind him.

"Move." Eric ordered. Ryker, legally being Eric's property, eased away from the door.

Eric opened the closet door to find a medium sized puppy sitting on a blanket, tail wagging. It was black mixed with two different shades of gray.

"What is that?" Eric demanded. The puppy barked at him, revealing large teeth, too big for a regular dog.

"A puppy." Ryker answered. He eased past Eric and picked the dog up. The puppy licked his face and its tail started wagging.

"Obviously I know that. Why is it here?" Eric shut the wardrobe door and spun around.

"He's not an it. He's a puppy." Ryker argued. He sat on the floor with the puppy in his lap.

"Yeah, a puppy dire wolf." Gilbert remarked.

"A dire wolf!?" Both Adaline and Eric exclaimed.

"Whose side are you on, Gilbert?" Ryker retorted. Gilbert shrugged in reply

"You cannot have a pet dire wolf!" Eric yelled. The dire wolf growled from Rykers lap. It clearly hated Eric raising his voice just as much as Ryker did.

"Eric." Gilbert sat up. "You don't need to yell. Let me explain."

"Yeah. I thought you lost that temper of yours ages ago." Adaline admonished as her eyebrows rose.

"We found that pup in the forest before we made it into the city. It was the only one of its litters that survived, and its mother didn't survive either." Gilbert explained. "We couldn't just leave him."

"Well, with that being said, what's his name?" Adaline asked, taking a seat across from Gilbert. Ryker's eyes lit up.

Eric knew he was probably not going to win the argument, not with all three of them against him, but that wasn't going to stop him from trying.

"Hold on, let's not make any hasty decisions." Ryker's face fell. "Don't pout at me, Ryker. Let's be smart about this. Dogs cost money to raise. How do you plan to pay for it?"

"Take it out of my salary." Ryker released the squirming puppy from his arms.

"Ryker, I own you. You don't have a salary." Eric watched the wolf pup strut over to Gilbert and start tugging on his pants leg.

"Aw man, I almost got away with that." Ryker started pouting again. Gilbert chortled, though Eric couldn't tell if it was at Ryker, or at the wolf pulling at his trousers.

"No, you didn't!" Eric exclaimed.

"I'll help pay for it." Adaline chimed in.

"Me too." Gilbert agreed as he picked up the wolf and set it in his lap.

"See? They'll help. Can I keep him? Please?" Ryker pleaded. He was such a child. Then again, he didn't have much of a childhood, so perhaps he was compensating.

"Fine, but you must train him yourself, you'll feed him yourself and if he destroys anything in my office or jeopardizes this mission, you'll have to answer for that yourself." Eric rolled his eyes as Ryker popped up and snatched the wolf from Gilbert. *It would seem it's not just Ryker. I'm surrounded by children.* Eric thought to himself

"His name is Bear! I've decided." The wolf started licking his face.

"A wolf named Bear? You can't be serious. That's stupid." Eric grumbled.

"What's wrong with a wolf named Bear?" Ryker sounded genuinely disappointed in his reaction. Gilbert cleared his throat and gave Eric a look.

"Fine. Fine! Name the thing whatever you want!" He threw his hands up in frustration. Ryker grinned, probably feeling too pleased with himself

Adaline took the wolf from his hands and set it on her lap as she sat back down.

Eric dug in his coat pocket and pulled out a bag of coins, which he promptly threw at Ryker. He was too distracted by his new pet to see it coming and it bounced off his head.

"Eric, that wasn't very nice." Gilbert scolded. He sounded like a mother telling her child to be nice to their sibling.

Ryker knelt down and picked up the coin purse.

"Go buy, *Bear* something to eat." He didn't like that name for a wolf, something like Alpha or Beta would be better, but he let Ryker have his fun.

Smile brimming, Ryker headed out the door. Eric looked at the wolf cub and Adaline's arms. *I suppose he would make a good security dog at the wyvern.*

Epilogue

Ryker

Ryker strolled around the empty streets. He'd decided to take a side route to the market, which according to Eric and Adaline, would still be open by now. The night sky was calming, so was the smell of rain still in the air. He enjoyed his time with the others, but he also enjoyed his time to himself.

He patted the coin purse in his left pocket, he'd never really been trusted with money before. He wondered how much was actually in the bag he was given, though it probably wasn't much. He couldn't see Eric trusting him with anything more than pocket change.

He yawned. He hated to admit it, but walking the entire way was draining. Not to mention the sprinting he'd needed to do in order to keep up with Gilbert.

He was back in a city, so it was more familiar, although the empty streets were something out of the normal.

In Hadune, people would stay up all night, drinking, gambling, anything to distract them from the work they had to do in the morning. Everything seemed quiet, almost too quiet.

The fine hairs on his neck stood on end. His hand drifted to a knife on his belt. The second he stopped to look around, something struck him in the side of the head.

The blow knocked him off his feet and onto his side, splashing in a rain puddle as he hit the ground. *Where did that come from?*

Coughing and trying to gather his wits, he rolled up to his hands and knees.

Someone grabbed the back of his neck and yanked him up off the ground. Panicking, squirming, and twisting, he desperately tried to get free.

"Let me go! Let m-*mph*!" Whoever it was stuffed a cloth over his mouth and nose.

An intoxicating scent filled his nostrils. Soon after Nausea and exhaustion hit him, and his struggles became sluggish. *No!*

His panic did little to help him fight off whoever had him, instead it only made his breathing more rapid, forcing him to inhale more of whatever was on the cloth. *Eric!*

He tried to send waves of distress through his necklace, like he'd done when Eric was trapped in the temple, but it very clearly wasn't working. Ryker wasn't a mage.

Should've traveled by roof. He thought just before everything went black.

Don't miss out!

Visit the website below and you can sign up to receive emails whenever Jazlynn Dickens publishes a new book. There's no charge and no obligation.

https://books2read.com/r/B-A-IDOMB-TFCJD

BOOKS 2 READ

Connecting independent readers to independent writers.

About the Publisher